THE DESERT

THE

DESERT

Allen Wheelis

BASIC BOOKS, INC., PUBLISHERS

New York / London

© 1969, 1970 by Allen Wheelis

Library of Congress Catalog Card Number: 72-110778

SBN   465-01604-9

Manufactured in the United States of America

Designed by Loretta Li

Portions of this book have appeared in Commentary,
May 1969, under the title "How People Change."

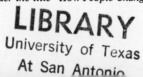

THE DESERT

I

In the beginning
was hydrogen. Then helium.
Atoms become larger,
become molecules, compounds.
Ever larger, more complicated,
through millions of years of chemical evolution,
become the proteins.

But chemistry is not yet life.

Life appears when one molecule
takes something in,
uses it to reproduce itself.
This is the minimum criterion,
necessary and sufficient.

A bit of the world is destroyed,
something new is created.
Destruction and creation are life.
Not the one or the other.
Both

II

For long the destructive process
is a taking something in and breaking it down,
the creative process
a splitting asunder.

As organisms become larger,
special parts evolve:
mouths with which to destroy,
sexual organs with which to create.

Only the first life fed on non-life.
Thereafter life feeds on life.
Rat destroys the grain,
hawk falls on hare,
bird takes worm,
wings flutter.
Small things struggle in the jaws of larger things.
Jaws develop fangs.
Big fish eat little fish.
Man eats grain, hare, fowl, fish, lamb.

Christ is said to have blessed
the three fishes and the loaves of bread,
but the blessing fell
not on cut wheat nor caught fish
but on the multitude which devoured them.

III

Nothing comes from nothing.
The new gathers itself from the body of the old.
Mushrooms spring drunkenly from the rotten trunk,
cancer sprouts on the dying breast.
The ethereal leap of the ballerina
is fueled by the flesh of a steer.

We are both predator and victim.
As plants of the field develop thorns
the teeth of grazing animals become stronger.
As the antelope becomes more fleet,
the stalking lion grows stealthy,
his claws more sharp.

Without destruction there is no creation.
Let those who praise life know they praise equally
the destroying and the creating.

IV

As organisms become more complicated
their destroying goes beyond incorporation,
their creating transcends reproduction.
Something new has entered the circus of life.

We kill men who have more to eat than we,
or who threaten to take what we have,
or who do not threaten
but whom we so imagine.

We kill to take the female or the territory of a rival.
A rival is one who
has a female or a territory we desire.
This is said to be good in the long run,
yielding offspring less likely to be eaten.
So we grow stronger,
so we endure and prevail.

Property is a function of the willingness to fight.
Titles are written in blood.
Dusty deeds rest on old murders.

V

Sometimes we kill for fun.
Faces upturned, Romans watch their Emperor in golden robes
cavort on the Temple of Saturn.
He throws coins which they scramble to gather.
Now he throws a knife.
A woman screams.

VI

Mouths fit on mouths,
eyes close,
tongues seek and come close
but never quite reach the yearning stranger.
Penises push forever in the dark cave,
push and spit
but reach no light.

We are children of slime,
we live on others,
our teeth break bones, suck marrow.

Where are the angels?

VII

Flesh no longer suffices,
we live also on spirit.
We kill men who threaten our holy faiths—
Sun God, Christ, white skin, free enterprise—
or who do not threaten
but whom we so imagine.

VIII

Man lives in ever larger aggregates—
communities, tribes, nations—
with special groups to destroy
and others to create.

Everyone eats but few kill.
Technicians fell the lamb.
Eating becomes a ceremony of innocence,
tinkle of crystal, rustle of taffeta.
Teeth are for beauty.
Visit every restaurant in town,
never pass the house of slaughter.

Leather shoes and belt,
mink coat, alligator handbag, gloves of calf,
lizard watch bands, peacock feathers—
how we deck ourselves in the skins and scraps!—
yet never strike a blow
nor cut a throat.

We push away our own destructiveness,
make it alien,
become finally unaware,
see only the destructiveness of others.

IX

The tendency of civilization
is not to eliminate destructiveness,
nor even diminish it,
but to remove it.

Tooth to hand to stone to blade to bullet to bomb—
so man estranges himself from his victim.
Our fate falls now from the touch of a finger
in a cave of ice.

X

Those who create the images we live by
stand most aloof from the destructiveness
by which, equally, we live.
Poet and philosopher sit to meat,
speak of love, charity,
rights of man, sacredness of life.
Far away blood flows,
cries rise in the night.
They benefit from such order as our cities afford
but it's the cop on the beat
who pistol-whips the thug.

They are heirs to the affluent society,
the museums, universities, theaters, libraries
of an armed sovereign state,
but it's the soldier who fights the wars
which that state, however mistakenly,
considers necessary for its survival.

So it comes about that
those who tell us what life should be,
who create our image,
find killing to be ugly, mean,
and set about in their dismay
to draw maps of human nature
in which destruction has no primary place,
to make songs, poems, world views, religions
which portray killing as unnecessary,
a kind of waywardness or error into which we have fallen,
from which, by these creations of theirs,
we must be rescued.

Such maps become new justifications
for more extensive killings.
Holocausts
are in the name of peace, freedom, justice, truth.

XI

The anguish of the Circus Maximus reappears
at but a greater distance
in the vision of the Last Judgment.

It reappears quite immediately—
with a violence greater by far than that of the Circus—
in the Holy Inquisition
and the Thirty Years' War.

XII

Shall we mourn the lost verities?
the wasteland of value
whence drift the winds of our despair?
How may we be saved
if nothing is worth dying for?

It is not true, brother.
We in our time are as willing as any men ever
to kill and be killed for what we hold dear.
Values drove the Third Crusade,
offered up the crimson-blooded Aztecs,
inspired the Terror,
filled the ovens at Auschwitz,
exploded the bomb over Hiroshima.
Values have value for those who find them valuable;
we suffer no dearth of spiritual commodity.

Nor find we fault with values as such.
True values are altogether beneficial.
Only false values cause trouble.
Fortunately we can unerringly distinguish:
true values are the ones we hold;
false values are those which oppose our own.

We indicate false values
by giving them special names:
superstition, ignorance, barbarism.
People who hold false values are known as enemies.
The correct way of spreading true values is violence.
Upon this all are agreed.

Were values disappearing we should rejoice, brother,
but they are not.
Old ones fade but new ones emerge
bright and convincing,
serve just as well for the killing and being killed
which is our traditional way of life.
Would that the passion of value
might subside to the preference of taste.
Would that commitment
might become so pallid.

Would we then,
bereft of death by violence,
die of boredom?

XIII

We destroy and we create.
Monuments of murder and of creation
reach to heaven.
We come now to a time
when our capacity to tear down
dazzles our capacity to build.

Conscience is the mandate of the group
installed in one beating heart,
enforces murder and brotherhood
with equal authority.

Hydrogen warheads sleep lightly in underground nests.

Kyrie, eleison. Christe, eleison. Requiem aeternam.

I

We have not far to look for suffering. It's in the streets,
fills the air, lies upon our friends. Faces of pain look at us
from newspaper, from TV screen. We know them: black
man swinging in the warm wind, sealed cattle cars
rumbling through the bitter cold, the glare of Auschwitz at
midnight, the sweet smell.

And then there's always the suffering inside. But that's
different. It may be very bad, this private misery, but
different.

For many people pain is imposed, there's no escape. It
may be impersonal, unavoidable, as by fire, flood, cancer;
or man-made, as in wars, sack of cities, rape of girls.
Victims still have choice; there's always a little corner of
freedom. They may throw spears at the bombers or bow in
prayer, may curse or plead; but they may not choose to
suffer or not suffer. That choice has been foreclosed.
Starving blacks of Biafra scrounge for roots, fight each other
for rats; Vietnamese children with melted flesh wander
homeless, orphaned, across a lunar desert.

Many of us have never known this kind of misery, have
never felt a lash or club, never been shot at, persecuted,
bombed, starved—yet we suffer too. Wealth and
intelligence and good fortune are no protection. Having had
good parents helps but guarantees nothing; misery comes
equally to high born and low, comes with the gold spoon,
to prince and princess and ladies-in-waiting, to groom and
gamekeeper, to the mighty and the humble. We feel our
suffering as alien, desperately unwanted, yet nothing

imposes it. We eat, often exceedingly well; the roof over
our head is timber and tile; we know deep carpets, thin
china, great music, rare wine; a woman looks at us with
love; we have friends, families; our needs are met. In some
way, unnoticed, unknown, we must elect our suffering,
create it. It may be quite intense.

Some of it is public knowledge—madness, suicide,
running amuck. Some of it is visible only to a few, to
family and friends who see the withdrawal, depression, the
sense of rejection, the clawing competitiveness, the bitter
frustration, bafflement and anger, year after year after year.
At the concert or opera, walking about in the lobby, we
bow, we smile, we glitter—show nothing of the misery
inside. And some of our suffering is altogether private,
known to no one but him who suffers, not even his wife, is
borne with shame as some indescribable awkwardness in
living, a kind of disloyalty to life to be in despair in the
midst of plenty.

Imposed suffering has priority over elected suffering, as
material needs take precedence over spiritual. "First feed
the belly, then talk right and wrong," says Mack the Knife.
Or Sartre: ". . . the exploitation of men by other men,
undernourishment—these make metaphysical unhappiness a
luxury and relegate it to second place. Hunger—now that *is*
an evil." Imposed suffering, therefore, protects from the
elected kind, crowds it out. We simply cannot create
despair from subjective roots if we are forced into despair
by persecution. In the concentration camp, states of created
despair are remembered vaguely as if from a different life,
discontinuous with the present one in which despair issues
from S.S. truncheons.

To those whose suffering is imposed, elected suffering
seems unreal. Lacking in measurable circumstance, in

objective explanation, it seems illusory, made up, "in the head." Victims of the whip feel envy of those so sheltered from pain as to be able to dream up states of misery; contempt when such fortunate ones have the arrogance to elegize their torment; a hateful mirth at existential despair hatching in a nest of IBM stock certificates.

We who compose our own misery are ambivalent toward victims of imposed suffering. We feel a subtle pride—secret, never expressed, unknown often even to ourselves—that our misery is more complicated, spiritual; as if we whispered, "The pain of being hungry, of being beaten, is very bad, we sympathize, will make a contribution to CARE; but it is, after all, a primitive suffering; anyone can feel it; just leave them alone, give them enough to eat, and they'd be happy—whereas only a poet could feel what I feel." At the same time, more openly felt, more easily expressed, we feel shame, judge our created misery to be petty in comparison.

In fact they are equally bad: depression or starvation is a hard choice; the terror of the ledge ten floors up matches the terror of the firing squad. In felt experience, that is: in worthiness we cannot call them equal. We who compose our own misery are ashamed at Babi Yar, at Nagasaki, on the slave ships from Africa, in the arena at Rome. They were innocent of their suffering, we are guilty of complicity with ours; they had no choice in theirs, we bear responsibility for ours.

Created suffering, except where precluded by imposed pain, affects us all. The well-adjusted lie: listen to them at your risk; listen to them long enough, declaiming the official view, being serious with their slogans, and you lose contact with your own heart. Poets tell the truth: the sadness of Greece and Gethsemane, of Sodom and

Gomorrah, of the Pharaohs and their minions and their slaves was as our own. It's part of being human, we differ from one another only in more or less. A few tranquil ones, with little conflict, suffer less; at the other extreme, stretched by despair to some dreadful cracking point, one goes berserk. In between are the rest of us, not miserable enough to go mad or jump off the bridge, yet never able if we are honest to say that we have come to terms with life, are at peace with ourselves, that we are happy.

The older I get the less I know, the darker the well of time. The enigma grows more bleak. I seek.

Herewith are segments of the seeker's thought and scenes from the seeker's life. I am concerned with suffering and with change, and I write equally for patient and therapist. What one should know will be useful, also, to the other. Here psychotherapy parts company with medicine.

The book for the surgeon is not the book for the surgical patient. One delivers one's ailing body—with its abscess or tumor or broken bone—into the hands of the surgeon, and his most elementary information and skill will transcend anything the patient need know. The patient must cooperate—one green capsule three times a day, keep the leg elevated, force fluids—but need not understand how or why. The responsibility lies with the surgeon, the problem is his, his the accountability for failure, the credit for success. Patient and surgeon do not learn from the same text.

Many patients go to psychiatrists as if to surgeons, and many psychiatrists regard themselves as psychic surgeons. When such a patient comes to such a therapist a relationship of considerable length may result, but little else. For the job can be done, if at all, only by the patient. To assign this task to anyone else, however insightful or charismatic, is to disavow the source of change. In the process of personality change the role of the psychiatrist is catalytic. As a cause he is sometimes necessary, never sufficient. The responsibility of the patient does not end with free-associating, with being on time, with keeping at it, paying his bills, or any other element of cooperation. He is accountable only to himself and this accountability extends all the way to the change which is desired, the achieving of it or the giving up on it.

So—consider one who suffers. Perhaps a woman with a warm heart but frigid. What can she do? Perhaps a mother who wants to love her children but does not. Maybe a homosexual living an endless series of hostile transient encounters. Perhaps a man in his middle fifties with a depressive character, normal to his friends, but constantly brushing away cobweb thoughts of suicide, one who is bored, finds no meaning in life, is ashamed. Consider one who suffers—anyone you know well. Consider perhaps yourself.

II

The apartment building pinnacles above me, curved in
every dimension—in cross-section an arc, in elevation east
to west an unstrung bow, north to south a convex lens—
thirty-six floors of glass with steel meridians converging top
and bottom. At the entrance in a bed of red canna lilies a
granite boulder with a gilded plaque: " 'A barrel stave
from heaven by the great Cooper for the people of San
Francisco.' Mayor William S. Burlingame, presenting the
Planned Parenthood Award to architect Samuel P.
Farberitz." The lobby is lead-colored flags, rubber trees,
split-leaf rhododendrons. Through glass doors a large
swimming pool with purple hydrangeas, red oleanders,
pink azaleas, and four girls in bikinis practicing the can-can
on the pool edge, while below them treading water a
young man with red beard and movie camera photographs
the scissoring thighs. A doorman in black uniform with red
stripes and gold epaulets examines my invitation, admits
me. A young man in gold uniform and gold pillbox hat
directs me to a tapestried panel which opens suddenly to
become an elevator. I find myself alone in a rapidly
ascending truncated cone—deep red carpeting on the floor,
red velvet on the ceiling, gilded double eagles on the
walls; from a concealed speaker Viennese waltzes; gold
telephone; two gold buttons marked "floral" and "musk." I
push "floral" and leap back, cracking my head on an eagle,
enveloped in a hissing spray of perfume.

The elevator stops, the door opens noiselessly upon a
tremendous curved room, one wall of arced glass covered

with transparent white gauze through which I see the blue bay, white sails, and a great tanker slipping by low in the water. On a platform, trumpet erect against the sky, a Negro creates an ear-splitting shriek. People are dancing, girls in gold leotards carry trays of hot hors d'oeuvres.

"Oh, darling!" A young woman hugging a black Persian cat rushes toward me. She has large blue eyes with exceedingly long lashes, on her upper lids a purple shadow with flecks of gold. Her skin is rosy, her mouth full and red, on her left cheek a black spot, her hair a cascade of white curls. "You don't recognize me!" Still holding the cat, she hugs me; the cat, caught between us, miaows and claws me. "Oh, you poor, poor sweetheart," she says to the cat. "Did I squeeze my darling Mister too hard?" I realize with amazement this is Ellen, my hostess, who has short brown hair. To me she says, "You smell like a rose. Darling, come, come, I simply have to talk to you." She takes my hand, leads me through crowds of people into a bedroom, stands facing me, hugging the cat with both arms. "I'm so shy! My dear, you can see *everything*. Look!" She drops the cat on the bed, opens her arms. From the waist up she wears one layer of black chiffon. "You can see *everything*," she repeats. "Look." She points to a small mole just above her left nipple. "What do you think? Is it too too awful?" "Charming," I say. She laughs. "Oh, I'm so shy. I'll simply have to hold Mister all evening." She picks up the cat, hugs him, kisses him. "And he gets *so* impatient, don't you, darling?" She pets the cat, teases him, and the cat begins to play with her nipple, slaps it lightly with its paw; the nipple responds. "Oh, naughty, naughty!" She turns to me. "Did you see what he did? Isn't that the naughtiest thing? He's the naughtiest man here—aren't you, Mister?" Again she drops the cat to the bed, throws back her arms and shoulders, faces me. "Is it too too daring? . . . Oh, I just can't bear it. I'll probably have to change." She picks up Mister again and, holding him lightly at her hip, takes my hand, leads me back to the big room.

"It's a high A," someone says of the trumpet. In the foreground is the rattle of drums, bass, piano, the singer. All sounds compete; people shriek to be heard. The steely note of the trumpet is ceaseless, at times faint, at times, finding place in a melody, very loud, but never stops. When one trumpeter drops it another takes it up. When the combo finishes a tune and takes a rest, the trumpet continues. It's the sound of a jangled nerve, a riven tooth, a razor blade on glass, a fingernail crossing an endless blackboard.

Standing alone far from the orchestra is a slender dark woman with a look of pain. She watches the sailboats as if wishing herself away. Through crowds I manage to reach her, find myself shouting to be heard. She looks at me intently, reading my lips, unsmiling; when she speaks she brings her mouth close to my ear. I note her grave manner, her unwillingness to shout. I think we have met but she doesn't remember me. Neither of us can hear what the other says.

Someone pulls me away; when I'm free I can't find her. I come upon two friends at the bar on high gilded stools, before them slender glasses a foot high with orange-colored drinks, mint and cherries. Julian Miles has close-cropped gray hair, tanned sensual face, light blue eyes. Lars Monroe is six and a half feet tall, large handsome head, broad shoulders, thick chest, pale skin, eyes watery and bloodshot. He slumps, examines his fingernails. They are talking about Julian's new Masserati. Impossible to hear. Julian shouts,

Lars shakes his head. Julian takes us by the arms, leads us down the hall, into a closet.

"Terrible racket," he says. "Snobbery once removed . . . that's what I was saying. Those cheap cars, that '56 Ford of yours . . . you make a show of not making a show. I *had* to buy an expensive car—to disengage myself from your inverted ostentation."

"Very funny," Lars says. "It's good for picking up girls, that's all."

"You sound envious," Julian says. "Oh, by the way, who in the Institute has a new patient? A blonde?"

Lars shrugs. "Why?"

"When I drove up this morning . . . a real knockout. Great mass of hair wrapped around her head in some complicated way. Like a halo, fine as silk."

"My God," Lars says to me, "listen to that."

"Beige blouse," Julian continues, "chocolate skirt, great trembling breasts that bounced with each step."

"You noticed a great deal," I say.

"Everything. I slammed on the brakes. She was on the sidewalk. Blushed very pretty. Then I went around the block, came up behind: small waist, long elegant legs, plump little popo . . . ah *bellissimo!*" He pauses, looks the hungry gourmet. "Of most women," he says, "sexuality is only a part; of a few it's all. These rare ones are a pure distillate of sex. Everything—voice, gait, speech, manner, everything—announces a sexual presence. This is such a woman."

"Probably a hysteric and frigid," Lars says.

"Ah, *mon vieux,*" Julian says, "if hers is the face of winter there is in prospect for some lucky, lucky man—a marvelous thaw."

Lars snorts, leaves the closet. Julian and I return to the

bar, sit on the high gold stools, drink vodka. After a while Julian turns to me. "How *are* you?" I say. "Fine, fine," he shouts, radiant smile, flashing teeth. A musing look comes to his eye, a trace of cunning. He lays hand lightly on my arm, takes me from the bar.

"Listen to this," he says in the hallway, but still I can't hear. He leads me around a corner, pushes open a door. "No . . . not this one," he says, laughing and backing out. Before the door closes I see a bald-headed man with a fringe of gray hair, fully dressed, heaving atop a naked Negro girl on a white circular bed. Further down the hall Julian pushes another door, which turns out to be a bathroom; here we can talk.

". . . really the most beautiful deal," he says. "Listen. . . . I play golf with a doctor, about sixty, never made much money. Thirty years ago somebody gave him a thousand acres near Sunnyvale to settle a $10,000 debt. Can you imagine! Now it's surrounded by industrial plants, worth a million. He's in a bind. If he sells, right away he pays a quarter million in capital gains. Then . . . suppose he dies without having spent much of the rest, his son pays another half million in inheritance tax. The whole thing is pretty much shot. He can't stand stand it: he holds the land, taxes go up, he has to keep working. It's a millstone. No income, just ulcers, misery, hypertension. I send him to my broker. Listen. Here's the deal.

"He deeds the land to his son in exchange for an annuity contract guaranteeing $5,000 a month for life. That's it. Simple. But what fringe benefits! He doesn't pay any capital gains, it's an exchange of one kind of property for another. The son sells the land for a million dollars; he pays no capital gains either, he sells for what it was worth when he got it. No gift tax, there wasn't any gift. With a million dollars the son guarantees the annuity, puts the whole thing in mutual funds. My friend gets $60,000 a year as long as he lives. Nothing to worry about. When he dies the investment will be intact, more likely increased . . . unencumbered property for the son. No inheritance tax, there wasn't any inheritance. Isn't that a beaut?"

A look of profound musing hunger comes to Julian's face. He moistens his lips, swallows.

We leave the bathroom, rejoin the crowd. Far across the curved room I see the dark-haired woman. She is alone, examines drawings on the wall. When she turns I'm startled by the look of pain, go toward her, am stopped by an extended leg. "Hey, Max! How are you?" It's Ray Hunter at a small table with a large woman I don't know. He pulls me down in the empty place between them. "Hey, Max!" he shouts. "I've got a great idea." He makes sure the lady is listening, leans far over the table, which almost falls. "It'll make a million. Really! You can still buy in. Didn't know I was an inventor, did you? Surprised, aren't you? Well, here it is. . . . Ready?" Again he glances at the lady, puts a finger to his mouth. "Zipper wax!" he explodes, roars with laughter. "Sell it in movies so you can open your pants without making any noise. It's bigger than popcorn." The woman opens her eyes wide, then her mouth. "Ha! ha! ha! Ray, you're incredible! Ray, you're a card! You're out of this world!"

I get away, look for the dark-haired woman. Can't find her. It's night now, drops of water appear on the curved glass. The steely trumpet continues. Many people have left, those who remain are drunk, some sleep on the floor. I sit at the bar and drink. People join me, talk, leave. The trumpet is a great idea, makes conversation impossible, relieves the stress of ordinary parties where one hears just enough to struggle, hopelessly, toward communication. A woman with chemical hair sits beside me, faint scars on her throat. Anguished eyes fix on mine, eyelids are thin and papery, a million wrinkles. The mouth opens, closes, spreads out, becomes oval, puckers; wrinkles come and go. I hear nothing, she talks behind acoustic glass. The mouth stops, assumes a fixed smile; it's my turn. "Of course," I say, nodding, "Alaska had a severe winter. Russia too. In Minsk a thousand goats froze to death on the imperial tennis courts." She nods, smiles nervously, steps down. I'm not ready to let her go. "They stood there," I add portentously, "stone hard . . . till Easter, when they were butchered . . . served up to tennis players as hamburger." I smile, she smiles, we shake hands, she leaves, nodding graciously. We have enjoyed our chat, are happy in our new acquaintance.

More people sit with me. We drink, I watch their mouths, their eyes search mine. I no longer try to hear, I love that trumpet. A man with a wooden leg pulls himself onto a stool. He has a cane, pulls up his pants, hits the leg with his cane. His gray Vandyke beard bobs up and down, he orders a martini, toasts me; I toast his leg. When he leaves, a young lady in sandals joins me. She is nervous, keeps getting down from the stool, standing on one foot then the other, talks rapidly, looks about, points. I tell her about the severe winter in Minsk, but she has a literal mind, gives me pencil and paper from her purse. Now I'm lost. How do you do these things in writing? She looks on me adoringly—has she asked for my autograph? the greatest invention of our time?—moves from one foot to the other— where the bathroom is? or who led the march from Selma? I take the pencil and write, "(1) Max Archer, (2) The pill, (3) Down the hall, first door on the left, (4) Martin Luther

King." She is delighted, giggles, waves good-bye, shows it to a friend, points to me. They laugh, both wave, I wave back.

I have another drink. A woman with loose brown hair has trouble mounting the stool. I help her. She is soft and pretty, a bit plump, wears an orange jersey dress, skintight, nothing under. Good breasts to stand up so well, nipples outline themselves through the fabric. We don't talk, but communicate well. She leans against me, tilts back her head, closes her eyes as I come down on her mouth. For one so out of it her tongue is quick. She holds me tight and we almost fall. I begin to respond, lift her down, lead her to the hall. Every room is occupied by sleepers and fornicators. "Let's get out of here." She nods. We find her coat in a pile on the floor of a bedroom, while on the bed partly covered by more coats a couple, slowly having intercourse, pay no attention to us.

Outside a light rain is falling. She holds tight to my arm. I have difficulty recalling where I left my car, find it eventually, start toward my apartment. She is singing. "Let's go swimming," she says suddenly. "No." "Oh yes, yes! Let's swim . . . in the ocean. 'swun . . . der . . . ful!" She grabs the wheel. I object, she insists, I drive out Geary to the beach. She opens the door as we stop, drops her coat, runs down the concrete steps. I follow reluctantly. Into the water up to her knees she screams at the cold, but goes farther. A wave crashes over her, and she comes out drenched, into my arms. I want her there on the sand, but she is shaking. In the light as I open the car door she appears nude; the dress has become transparent, clings to her belly, outlines navel, brush of hair. I lock the door, she clings to me. "What's your name?" I ask. "Violet," she says, and I stifle a crazy laugh. She opens her legs, and we are caught in headlights. More cars are coming. I start the motor, drive toward Land's End, looking for a dark place. A light rain falls through the headlights in vertical slivers, glistens on the black road. No moon, no stars; on the short winding road we pass no car.

Suddenly there is a mass of flares, police cars, ambulance. Two wreckers are drawn up to the edge of the cliff, spotlights trained below. A police officer with red flashlight orders me to pull over. Nearby, in the headlights of a car, two men talk to another officer. A segment of railing is torn away at the edge of the cliff.

I open the door. "Wait here," I say to Violet. "I'm frightened," she says; "let me. . . ." She jumps out, buttons her coat, holds my arm with both hands. There is a smell of rubber, on the wet asphalt the black marks of tires. A police officer turns toward us, shrugs, says nothing. A hundred feet below, far out from the cliff, is a black convertible. It must have been going fast to go so far, and must have struck several times, for one of the doors is at some distance and two wheels are missing. It lies on its side on the furthermost rocks by the sea. Nearby, a white sidewall tire rises and falls in the water. Two men in black raincoats are doing something about the car, moving slowly; a third sits on a rock unfolding a stretcher. All are caught in the glare of spotlights. Violet moans, clutches my arm, hides her face. The ambulance leaves.

The body must be wedged in, for it takes a long time. Sea spray falls over the crushed car, the working men. Finally the body is free, strapped in a stretcher. A helicopter arrives, hovers with throbbing clatter, the wash of its blades making black water white. Violet shrinks back. Her hair is soaked, water runs from her face and neck, her hands move constantly on the buttons of her coat, "No, no, no, no . . ." she whispers.

The stretcher is pulled up in the night on a thread of bright cable, the bay doors open, the clattering monster receives the body. The racket increases and the machine rises. For a moment it hovers, as if looking for other prey, leans to one side, whirls away. Violet is moaning, her hands fumbling against me, small wounded animals.

III

I wake with pain, wish I'd said no to that third drink. Or
was it the fifth? Doesn't matter. To bed early, to bed late;
one drink, five drinks, no drinks—pretty much the same,
always that aching of back and limbs, that horror of
climbing up into awareness. It's not the parties, but the
getting old perhaps. I push legs out of bed, lurch into the
day, shave, dress, drink black coffee.

In the anteroom I unlock the door to the hall, enter the
living room, which is also my office. Thirteen floors up in a
tower on Russian Hill. The fog comes up to my glass walls,
seals me in white silence. I am cut loose from the world,
can't see the street below. A buzzer announces my first
patient. I check my appearance in the mirror: gray check
shirt, gray silk knit tie, charcoal flannel suit, graying hair,
inscrutable gray eyes, a man of distinction, an air of calm.
No longer the defiant outcast—I've not so much given up
the role, as been forced out of it by my patients who have
a better claim. However unfitting, I now am representative
to them of that larger society with which they must come
to terms, in which my place is assumed to be secure,
responsible.

Desk is covered with papers, books, letters. Across the
room a couch of gray ribbed fabric, pillow hollowed like
stone before old altars, double doors to hold in secrets and
weeping and anger, black leather chair with ottoman
where I sit out of sight behind the couch, two walls of
books, two walls of glass.
I go to the anteroom, pause, brace myself, open the

door. A small woman, gaunt, tense as a steel spring, stands instantly. "Good morning, Mrs. Orley." She nods, bullets in with lowered eyes, the same misery as when she left on Friday. She passes before me, I close the double doors. Already on the couch, gaze fixed on ceiling, she does not watch as I cross the room, launches immediately on her sorrows. She will not reach the end in fifty minutes.

I listen for a while, then wander. Across the room are a stack of offprints. "Introjects in the Ego" was my last and best, but I feel no pride. A scurrying about in the darkness of soul trying to catch some psychological game. They snared nothing that lived, lie there on the shelf, broken traps.

I recall myself to Mrs. Orley, listen to her troubles, drift off again. She is content to talk without response but it is easier for me to attend if I am active, so I interrupt to ask questions, become engaged by her replies, make an interpretation. When the hour is over I stand at the glass wall, look out into the cotton wool. I know I'm a prisoner because I stand so often in the posture of one who ponders escape. Yet there was a time, and not so long ago, when a room like this—analytic chair bearing the marks of silent listening, couch beginning to sag, pillow depressed by anguished heads ("Here we go again," one of my weeping women said, "tears in my ears . . . for years . . . it's like a song")—had seemed a frontier outpost from which explorations into the unknown were provisioned and launched.

Next comes Mrs. Laine, whose analysis is being recorded on tape for research, a gray-haired woman, obsessional, depressed, came to me after an attempt at drowning herself. She has a face once pretty, now worried, with brooding, absent eyes. She strokes her chin, and in the middle of an hour will start up and say, "I forgot to lock the front door, I guess it's too late now?. . ." or "I forgot to put a dime in the parking meter. Well, I guess it's too late. . . ." "Oh, I forgot to turn off the oven. The roast will be ruined." Today while talking of her daughter's wedding ten years ago, "Oh, I forgot to thank Susan for the silver platter. I guess it's too late." Whenever something important looms, "Oh, I forgot!" and she never gets back. Once her husband said in exasperation, "Even in bed . . . I'll get interested, then, 'Oh, I forgot to turn off the heater, I guess it's too late. . . .' She's going to forget her own funeral, then it really will be too late."

Another patient, then another and another, lunch, and back at the window, leaning against the frame, looking out, three more patients, and I'm through, thank God. At a quarter of four I'm on my way to the Federalist Institute, up four flights, and there . . .

. . . twenty tables, twenty boards, overflowing ashtrays, lowered heads, gray hair, brown hair, bald; on the shelf books by Lasker, Nimzovitch, Capablanca; on the walls old photographs turning yellow, Morphy, Steinitz, Anderson, and Dr. Tarasch, who wrote that ". . . chess, like love, like music, has the power to make men happy," but it's not true and we all know it, it is rather like dueling with sabers, the point and cutting edge of one intelligence applied to another, to run through, to slice, to annihilate, and no happiness in that for anyone; chess room open every day including Christmas, and always players, taciturn, bland, garrulous, or grim; dapper men with tightly knotted ties, truck drivers in undershirts, neat accountants, depressed lawyers, retired doctors, pimply students, chess bums with elbows coming through ragged jackets; the alienated, the severely estranged, occasionally the outright schizophrenic, coming back day after day to create from an otherwise impotent fury formal patterns of force and destruction, thereby perhaps avoiding madness but just barely, finding no peace, no lasting triumph, because there's always a stronger player; the anger of kings breaking out of checkered realms, a piece slammed on a board, a shrill voice breaking the silence, "No! You touched the rook! You touched the rook . . . No . . . No . . . I insist! . . . No . . . No . . . Move the rook!" Appalled at such fury, at finding myself here, knowing that art is a social act and commitment that draws people together, while this game however artfully played is but the art of Napoleon and Rommel; sitting down nevertheless, the addict, and what shall it be today?—Ruy Lopez, Queen's Pawn Game, Giucco Piano?—deciding on a new line in the Max Lange attack, the engulfing preoccupation, straining to see the combination; the chagrin, even nausea, of blunder; pulling out of it finally and winning in the end game by a pawn; looking up at six-thirty to an implacable fury on the deeply lined face of an intelligent paranoid bum with a three-day beard and chronic malnutrition. For a moment his hatred shines forth like a floodlight; then the eyes cloud over, he farts, and with a casual brush of his arm sweeps aside the remaining pieces, mumbles something, leaves.

For a few minutes I stand at the window, look down on the frantic twilight traffic, exhaust fumes, twinkling lights, then drive to the psychoanalytic institute, meet Julian in the hall. A woman in a green silk dress, tight as a glove, walks ahead of us, her mincing gait bunching and revealing one buttock after the other. Julian makes a gesture of speechless admiration. "Marvelous!" he breathes. "Incredible! So simple . . . such elemental beauty!" The door to Lars's office is open. We enter. Lars is in shirtsleeves, tie loosened, collar unbuttoned, baggy brown pants, jacket on the couch as if thrown. He has developed a paunch which his belt supports, a bald spot on the back of his head which almost touches the low ceiling. He is pacing slowly about the small office, frowning, occasionally strikes his left palm with his right fist, is talking to Dr. Clive Milton, who was once our teacher. Clive has thin gray hair brushed back close to his head, swarthy, unwrinkled skin, wears rimless glasses which he never removes, never plays with. He has been asking Lars, I gather, to take on some additional task in our research. "The whole idea makes me tired," Lars says angrily. "I don't know whether it's any good or not, but I have no confidence." He resumes walking. "This kind of project is promising only in prospect. As soon as you start, it becomes meaningless. We throw out what we can't agree on, which is the heart of the matter, affirm what we do agree on, which is something everybody knows anyway. Of course," he says, with a sudden grin, "it might demonstrate the impossibility of verification in analysis, and *that* would be important . . . but wouldn't come to light, would be just one more thing we couldn't agree on."

Julian stands at the window, aloof, watches the woman in the green dress get in her car.

"You know something?" Lars goes on. "I could devise a project in which patients were fed"—his glance falls upon the recording machine on his desk—"extract of ground Audograph discs and show eighty percent cure—if I believed in it. What's more I could get a grant." He grins again. "Sometimes . . . I don't want to shock you, you know . . . sometimes I doubt that psychoanalysis has *any* therapeutic effect. Because, for one thing, all analysts have been analyzed, and you know how sick they are—present company excepted, you understand."

Clive turns to Julian, asks if he will summarize the research conferences. Julian smiles, declines. Lars tilts back in his chair, looks at the ceiling. "This project will take about two more years," he says slowly. "Another year to write it up. Then it will be published. I can picture it. A book with, say, a red cover. Three hundred pages. About like that one on the second shelf." He points across the room. "Gold lettering on the back: *The Therapeutic Process* by Milton, Archer, Miles, and Monroe. All the libraries will buy it. Many psychiatrists. All the social workers too . . . they're in the bag. Good title, will look good on office shelves." He grins at me. "And that's that . . . chaps!"

I remember those first few months of 1946, the three of us living together in an old army barracks in Topeka, eating together in the cafeteria, walking down those miles of corridors with the snow swirling outside, past the popping radiators, brown linoleum crackling underfoot, laughing together, cared for by the Veterans Administration as formerly by the army, carefree at the war being over, at being out of uniform and forever through with the military mind, at being students again, entering a vocation arrogantly aimed at the heart of all mysteries, interpreting everything—ourselves, each other, teachers, public figures— careless with newfound insights, excited at getting behind the scenes, up in the flies, looking down on the human condition. I listen to them argue now, watch darkness come . . . endless discussions, endless tapes . . . leave abruptly.

In Ghirardelli Square a crowd of people, photographers, floodlights. Pictures are being taken for a fashion magazine:

under a red and blue umbrella a laughing girl in a bikini; at some distance, another photographer and a tall, willowy girl with doe eyes and a generous mouth. I sit in the bar at Señor Pico's, have a martini. A waiter tells me my table is ready. I order another drink, don't want food, want a woman. As if I have rubbed a magic lamp, she appears.

Not a woman, a girl. Wears a sleeveless dress of green suede, sandals, no stockings, has dark skin, long black hair hanging loose to her waist. Very pretty, about nineteen, red lips. She glances at me, sits on the next stool, turns away to examine her makeup. I catch her eye in the mirror of her compact, admire the curve of her cheek, the toss of her head to shake out her hair. I want to touch her, say something tender, sensual. Dance for me, darling. Console me in the sweet motion of your hips, in the dark confusion of your flesh, for all our lost certainties.

She completes the check of appearance, adds a finishing stroke. The bartender waits for her order. She turns to me with an offer. "Hello!" she says, and I realize with dismay I don't want her. There's nothing wrong with her, I can see through suede: she got her tan without a bra, just a white gull-wing about her groin. It's me. I can't believe that this is it, that this will do. Watch out, I tell myself, you'll lose everything. I buy her a drink and leave, glance back to see her looking in the mirror, wondering why.

Outside I stand by an iron railing, look out over the bay. The fog is gone, it's a clear night with a warm wind. The moon makes a silver wake to Oakland. Before me the dark slopes of Angel Island. A ship passes. The lights of the city disappear. I see only shoreline, water, islands, the treeless hills. At a pay telephone I call Ellen. "It was a fabulous party," I say. "Oh, darling Max! How sweet of you!" "How's Mister?" "Oh, Max, he's the naughtiest. Won't leave me alone. You know what he did? Clawed a hole in my blouse—you saw how thin it was—right over my . . . you know! Isn't that scandalous? Then he . . ." I interrupt: "Ellen, there was a woman at your party . . . in a yellow dress. Alone. Very quiet. The trumpet seemed to bother her. Left early. You know who I mean?" "I've got bad news for you, darling. She's married, adores her husband." "What's her name?" "I'm just saving you time, honey. Why don't you come see me?" "What's her name?" ". . . You'll be sorry!" "What's her name?" "Ariana Craig."

IV

I live in a desert. Hour by hour feel myself dying. Surely I believe in something. Not much perhaps, but a little. What?

We are what we do . . . Identity is the integration of behavior. If a man claims to be honest we take him at his word. But if it should transpire that over the years he has been embezzling we unhesitatingly discard the identity he adopts in words and ascribe to him the identity defined by his acts. "He claims to be honest," we say, "but he's really a thief."

One theft, however, does not make a thief. One act of forthrightness does not establish frankness; one tormenting of a cat does not make a sadist, nor one rescue of a fledgling a savior. Action which defines a man, describes his character, is action which has been repeated over and over, and so has come in time to be a coherent and relatively independent mode of behavior. At first it may have been fumbling and uncertain, may have required attention, effort, will—as when one first drives a car, first makes love, first robs a bank, first stands up against injustice. If one perseveres on any such course it comes in time to require less effort, less attention, begins to function smoothly; its small component behaviors become integrated within a larger pattern which has an ongoing dynamism and cohesiveness, carries its own authority. Such a mode then pervades the entire person, permeates other modes, colors other qualities, in some sense is living and operative even when the action is not being performed, or even considered. A young man who learns to drive a car thinks differently thereby, feels differently; when he meets a pretty girl who lives fifty miles away, the encounter carries implications he could not have felt as a bus-rider. We may say, then, that he not only drives a car, but has *become* a driver. If the action is shoplifting, we say not only that he steals from stores but that he has *become* a shoplifter.

Such a mode of action tends to maintain itself, to resist change. A thief is one who steals; stealing extends and reinforces the identity of thief, which generates further thefts, which further strengthens and deepens the identity. So long as one lives, change is possible; but the longer such behavior is continued the more force and authority it acquires, the more it permeates other consonant modes, subordinates other conflicting modes; changing back becomes steadily more difficult; settling down to an honest job, living on one's earnings, becomes ever more unlikely. And what is said here of stealing applies equally to courage, cowardice, creativity, gambling, homosexuality, alcoholism, depression, or any other of the myriad ways of behaving, and hence of being. Identity is comprised of all such modes as may characterize a person, existing in varying degrees of integration and conflict. The greater the conflict the more unstable the identity; the more harmonious the various modes the more durable the identity.

The identity defined by action is present and past; it may also foretell the future, but not necessarily. Sometimes we act covertly, the eye does not notice the hand under the table, we construe the bribe to have been a gift, the running away to have been prudence, and so conceal from ourselves what we are. Then one day, perhaps, we drop the pretense, the illusion cracks. We have then the sense of an identity that has existed all along—and in some sense we knew it but would not let ourselves know that we knew it—but now we do, and in a blaze of frankness say, "My God! I really am a crook!" or "I really am a coward!" We may then go too far and conclude that this identity is our "nature," that it was writ in the stars or in the double helix, that it transcends experience, that our actual lives have been the fulfilling of a pre-existing pattern.

In fact it was writ only in our past choices. We are wise to believe it difficult to change, to recognize that character has a forward propulsion which tends to carry it unaltered into the future, but we need not believe it impossible to change. Our present and future choices may take us upon different courses which will in time comprise a different identity. It happens, sometimes, that the crook reforms, that the coward stands to fight.

. . . and may do what we choose. The identity defined by action is not, therefore, the whole person. Within us lies the potentiality for change, the freedom to choose other courses. When we admit that those "gifts" were bribes and say, "Well, then, I'm a crook," we have stated a fact, not a destiny; if we then invoke the leopard that can't change his spots, saying, "That's just the way I am, might as well accept it," we abandon the freedom to change and exploit what we have been in the past to avoid responsibility for what we shall be in the future.

Often we do not choose, but drift into those modes which eventually define us. Circumstances push and we yield. We did not choose to be what we have become, but gradually, imperceptibly became what we are by drifting into the doing of those things we now characteristically do. Freedom is not an objective attribute of life; alternatives without awareness yield no leeway. I open the door of my car, sit behind the wheel, and notice in a corner of vision an ant scurrying about on the smooth barren surface of the concrete parking lot, doomed momentarily to be crushed by one of the thousand passing wheels. There exists, however, a brilliant alternative for this gravely endangered creature: in a few minutes a woman will appear with a picnic basket and we shall drive to a sunny, hilltop meadow. This desperate ant has but to climb the wheel of my car to some sheltered ledge, and in a half hour will be in a paradise for ants. But this option, unknown, unknowable, yields no freedom to the ant, who is doomed; and the only irony belongs to me, who observes, who reflects that options potentially as meaningful to me as this one to this ant may at this moment be eluding my awareness; so I too may be doomed—this planet looks more like a parking lot every day.

Nothing guarantees freedom. It may never be achieved, or having been achieved may be lost. Alternatives go unnoticed; foreseeable consequences are not foreseen; we may not know what we have been, what we are, or what we are becoming. We are the bearers of consciousness but of not very much, may proceed through a whole life without awareness of that which would have meant the most, the freedom which has to be noticed to be real. Freedom is the awareness of alternatives and of the ability to choose. It is contingent upon consciousness, and so may be gained or lost, extended or diminished.

Modern psychiatry found its image in the course of dealing with symptoms experienced as alien. A patient so afflicted seeks no alteration of character or personality, would be offended if the physician suggested such or pretended to any competence in that area. Nothing is felt to be wrong with the patient as a person, his self is not presented for examination or treatment. He is a patient only because he's sick, and his sickness consists of an ailment of which he wishes to be relieved. If the trouble is of recent onset and condenses a specific conflict of impulse and inhibition the medical model may be tenable: insight may function as medicine and dispel the symptom. On those exceedingly rare occasions when we still see such a case, we can be real doctors again and cure someone. The following is an example.

A thirty-five-year-old woman suddenly, and for the first time in her life, develops a spasm of the right foot and a left-sided migraine. Brain tumor is suspected but neurological examination is normal. On psychiatric consultation it is learned that she has been married fifteen years, no children, is devoutly religious, cannot tolerate hostile feelings, but in fact despises her alcoholic husband. At a party, on the evening before her trouble began, she went upstairs looking for a bathroom and chanced upon her husband with a woman on his lap, the two of them in deep, prolonged kissing. She watched for a few moments, then backed out without being seen. On leaving the party, as her husband was drunk, she drove the car. Reaching home, he stumbled out to open the garage door and for a moment was caught in the headlights. Just beyond him was a concrete wall. The motor was idling fast. She felt dizzy, passed a hand over her face. Upstairs, a few minutes later, her right foot began to twitch; during the night she waked with a headache.

In this case, after certain preparations, the interpretation, "You wanted to kill your husband," may effect a cure. No will is necessary, no action, no change in being. Insight is enough.

Most psychiatrists know such cases only from reading

examples like this one. The patients who actually appear in their offices—whatever their symptoms—suffer problems of being. When the symptom is migraine it has occurred not once but hundreds of times, over many years. It is not the somatic expression of a specific conflict, but a response to any conflict, any tension, a way of running from whatever seems too much; it has become a mode of being in the world. The patient may feel it as alien, want to be rid of it, but it has become useful in a thousand unnoticed ways; its removal would not be simple relief but would expose the patient to conflicts which he has no other way of handling. The symptom does not afflict the patient, it *is* the patient.

This headache will not dissolve with insight, and here the medical model breaks down. What is called for is not cure of illness but change in what one is. Insight is not enough. Effort and will are crucial.

The most common illusion of patients and, strangely, even of experienced therapists, is that insight produces change; and the most common disappointment of therapy is that it does not. Insight is instrumental to change, often an essential component of the process, but does not directly achieve it. The most comprehensive and penetrating interpretation—true, relevant, well expressed, perfectly timed—may lie inert in the patient's mind; for he may always, if he be so inclined, say, "Yes, but it doesn't help." If a therapist takes the position, as many do, that a correct interpretation is one that gets results, that the getting of results is an essential criterion for the correctness of an interpretation, then he will be driven to more and more remote reconstructions of childhood events, will move further and further from present reality, responding always

41

to the patient's "Yes, but why?" with further reachings for more distant antecedents. The patient will be saying, in effect, "Yes, but what are you going to do about it?" and the therapist, instead of saying, as he should, "What are *you* going to do about it?" responds according to his professional overestimate of the efficacy of insight by struggling toward some ever more basic formulation. Some patients don't want to change, and when a therapist takes on the task of changing such a one he assumes a contest which the patient always wins. The magic of insight, of unconscious psychodynamics, proves no magic at all; the most marvelous interpretation falls useless—like a gold spoon from the hand of a petulant child who doesn't want his spinach.

An anguished woman enters our office, sits down, weeps, begins to talk, and we listen. We are supposed to know what's up here, what the problem *really* is, and what to do about it. But the theories with which we have mapped the soul don't help, the life she relates is unlike any other. We may nevertheless cling to our map, telling ourselves we know where we are and all is well, but if we look up into the jungle of her misery we know we are lost. And what have we to go on? What to cling to? That people may change, that one person can help another. That's all. Maybe that's enough.

The suffering is a given, but the problem is a choice, is subjective and arbitrary, rests finally upon nothing more than the patient's will, upon his being able to say "This . . . is what I want to change."

Those psychiatrists who regard themselves in the manner of medical men would disagree, would hold that a psychic problem—homosexuality, for example, or compulsivity—is objectively verifiable, that a panel of competent therapists would concur. This view would hold that the problem "emerges" from the "material," is recognized and defined by the therapist, who then presents it to the patient along with his recommendation for treatment.

But since a problem is something for which a solution is sought, only the patient can designate the problem. The therapist may perceive that a certain conflict leads regularly to such and such situations which cause suffering. But a cause of suffering is not a problem unless it is taken as such by the patient.

Likewise the goal of treatment must be determined by the patient. The only appropriate goal for the therapist is to assist. If the therapist cannot in good faith help to the end desired he is free to decline, but he cannot reasonably work toward goals of his own choosing. Even so benign a therapeutic aim as to "help the patient realize his potentials" may be too much. It is too much if that is not what the patient wants. Sometimes, indeed, the patient may want the opposite, may feel that his trouble comes from having begun to realize incompatible potentialities, and that from some of these he must now turn away.

V

I stand outside Enrico's in the warm sunshine, waiting. She
arrives on time, smiles. The small hand takes mine with
firm grip. We go inside to a secluded table, I take her
coat. She wears a pale blue sheath, entirely plain—no belt,
sleeves, or collar—blue jade earrings, has black hair drawn
back loosely, dark shell hairpins. Her eyes, under black
eyebrows, are grayish blue, like the earrings. I am struck
by the slender hand, by her seriousness and reserve, the
ease with which she looks at me.

"I think we have met," I say.

"No. I would remember you."

She declines a drink, we order lunch, talk slowly. I ask
about her. She is a painter, does not show. "I'm not that
good," she says. Her husband is in India making a film. "A
very gifted man," she says. I can't tell how she feels about
him. The brown hand lies close to mine on the white
marble. My knee seeks, does not find. She is remote,
castled on a mountaintop. I place my hand on hers. For a
few moments she allows this, then withdraws. Other
people enter the room. Lunch is over, she has an
appointment, thanks me, holds out her hand. "May I see
you again?" I say.

"Yes."

"I think you know why I wanted to meet you, but . . ."

"No, I don't," she says.

"At the party I watched you. We become grotesques.
You were the only one who didn't shout, who did not
change. I admire that."

She does not react, looks at me calmly, weighing what I have said. After a moment she accepts it. "I wanted to meet you," she says, "because I've read your book."

I'm surprised. It's not a book for laymen, is heavy going for professionals. "How did you happen to be interested?" I ask. She shakes her head, and for the first time I sense awkwardness.

"Since you know my work," I say, "will you let me see yours?"

"Yes."

I go north over the bridge to San Anselmo, leave Drake Highway, drive two miles on a winding road through redwood and eucalyptus, turn off on a narrow gravel road, come upon her house. It is on the lower slope of a high hill, white stucco with red tile roof, two stories high, pine trees, path covered with brown needles. Behind the house is an upsloping meadow beyond which is another building. A Negro woman answers the door, tells me Mrs. Craig is in her studio, directs me. Climbing a path through the meadow, I look down on the house, see that it encloses a patio with table and chairs.

The studio is unbroken walls of stone weathered to the satin gray of driftwood. The path leads around to the west side, the door is open. Ariana is at work before an easel, comes toward me with a smile, wiping her hands. "You're early. I'm glad. Come in." She wears black slacks, blue shirt with open collar. A number of paintings are standing about, many stacked against the walls.

It is a huge studio, perhaps thirty feet square, thirty feet high. Overhead are two steel beams with a movable crane. The roof is single pitch sloping up from south to north, entirely glass with several movable panels. There are no windows, but one small door and one set of double doors fifteen feet high. "It was built for a sculptor," Ariana says, watching me. I am touched by her slightness in this giant room, under this heavy equipment. "See!" She points to a block of uncut marble in a corner.

I begin to look at her work, oil on canvas, primitive, bright, vivid. "I will change while you look," she says.

I am alone in a massive cube of space. Nothing left of sculpture but the one block of marble, yet the mass of the building, the masonry walls, the rusting steel beams, the loops of heavy chain which hang from the crane, the rusting tracks in the timbered floor which lead to the double doors, evoke stone men on stone horses, stone hands on stone books, brooding stone faces.

What now occupies this space is a world of dwarfs, gnomes, animals. Many of the paintings are of odd shape and dimension: long panels with different scenes, L-shapes, curved boards, irregular patches of paper. One large picture frame, without a picture, is itself painted, portrays the death of a hunter: The hunter leaves home proudly, his dogs are tricked away by a stag, he is led into a black forest, is lost, a boar steals his gun, squirrels pelt him with nuts, beavers drop branches on him, he is toppled over a cliff, is borne away finally on the backs of animals with mock pomp to a funeral in a cave. In other paintings maidens with golden hair flee dragons breathing fire, gnomes build underground cities, witches convene at an IBM factory to study computers, a beached whale is engineered into the sea by dwarfs. All of them show devoted attention to detail, a childlike gravity. Blood flows red, birth and death are quick, everything is conflict, nothing ambiguous. Above all is the sense of things happening, of intense, bustling life.

I hear Ariana's voice, other sounds. After a while she

comes in, listens with attention to my impressions, says nothing, but I think is pleased. She takes me through a hidden door to a terrace of red flags surrounded by yellow and blue iris. There is a glass table with a bunch of violets, two chairs. We sit to a lunch of cold crab and white wine.

"You are so quiet," I say, "remote . . . I was not prepared . . . would have guessed, rather, pastel landscapes, miniatures, tiny brooks, bending willows—something light, ethereal."

"Isn't it your profession," she says, "to anticipate that people are not what they seem?" It is her first pleasantry with me, I am immensely amused.

After lunch we follow a path through the woods up the hill above the studio, pass a small cemetery, come at the top to a field of grass up to our knees bending and rustling in the wind, and far away to the west the blue ocean. I take her shoulders, kiss her on the mouth, am disappointed she does not respond.

"Why did you do that?" she says.

"Because I love you."

"Don't say that. I don't joke about love."

"What makes you think I'm joking?"

"The way you say it. Everything. Let's go."

"You know," I say, "I might just mean it."

She turns to me again. "What *do* you mean?"

The blue eyes, dark-framed, look at me so easily, with so honest an asking, that I am touched, now want desperately to kiss her again. Her hair moves in the wind. "I mean," I say, ". . . there's something about your hair that makes me want to touch it." I do so, surprised by its softness.

"That's what I thought you meant," she says in calm rebuke. "Come, let's go."

A week later I am back—with three dozen roses, red and

orange and yellow. Approaching the house, I hear impassioned, lyrical music: Mahler. Ariana opens the door. I enter a small hall with a low ceiling. Before me a stairway with wrought-iron railing leads to the second floor. To the right is a dining room, to the left a living room, whence the music. The floors are of waxed red tile, here and there a Caucasian rug. The walls are rough white plaster. She is pleased with the flowers, takes my arm, leads me into the living room. A fire is burning in the fireplace. Before it a small green sofa. She wears a black dress, a gold chain around her neck, no jewelry. Her arms and neck are bare. Watching her as she goes about arranging the flowers, I am struck by yearning, feel awkward. The music becomes pizzicato. I want to dance with her. The Negro woman, whose name is Emily, brings a pitcher of rum punch.

When we go in to dinner Ariana seats me at the end of the table, she on the side close to me. White candles burn in silver holders, cast shadows on walls; black walnut gleams through lace tablecloth. It is a room of low ceiling, dark beams, white shutters closed over black windows. I feel heady and festive, yet somehow confused and chastened. Several times I take her hand. "I love to be with you," I say.

After dinner Emily brings coffee to the living room. We sit on the green couch, look in the fire, say little. The fire burns low, there is a sighing from the pine trees. The French doors open suddenly to a gust of wind, and the gauze curtains billow into the room. Ariana looks up, her expression changes. "What's the matter?" I say. She shakes her head. "You remembered something," I suggest. "Tell me."
She seems for a moment to consider. "I was thinking of

my mother." She hesitates, then tells me with quickness and feeling.

"When she was home the windows and doors were open and the curtains would blow like that. She was always going away to sanitaria, coming home again, and the main thing I remember is how sad were the goings away, how happy the comings back."

She looks in the fire, smiles, touches my arm.

"On coming back she would be a stranger, but familiar, bending over me with loud, startling exclamations, sudden tears, furs that smelled of mothballs, crushing me against her, a scratch from a brooch with yellow stones—topaz— then she would swoop me up in a tingling of perfume and wild lips kissing me, crying out.

"And then, you know, the house would come to life. Everything would change: curtains would come down to be cleaned or replaced, blinds would open in dark rooms, my father would wander about pale and bewildered in the sunlight . . . but happy. Workmen would appear, painters, cleaning ladies with mops and sponges and waxes, strange smells, noises. Cobwebs would come down, floors would shine, windows sparkle; color would come back, bright silk runners on tables and chests, daffodils and roses and rust-colored chrysanthemums—she loved chrysanthemums—new pictures on the walls. The French doors to the terrace were always open, the wind would billow in the curtains— like that! In the parlor my mother would play waltzes from *Der Rosenkavalier* on a carved rosewood piano. Always music, and always, in those times, the music was a waltz."

Ariana is silent, continues slowly.

"Then one day I would realize the sounds had changed: the beat of heels had become nervous; no more waltzes but jazz or Wagner; sharp words between my mother and father; heavy silences; my mother's cough, always a lace handkerchief to her mouth. I would not know when it had started, but would feel it already far along, would think if I had noticed it sooner I might have stopped it, but knowing it was too late now, that nothing would stop it; and one day—I would feel it coming—she would burst into tears, rush to her room, and a few days later would be gone. I would be alone with my father in a still house, darker than before, flowers gone, vases empty, French doors closed on the garden, curtains hanging . . . motionless . . . dust appearing on floors and tables. . . ."

She is silent, observes presently her hand on my arm, fingers playing with the tweed of my jacket, smiles. "I've not thought of her like this for a long time."

I am moved by her confidence, want to give her something. I take her hand.

We hear the sound of a car. Ariana is puzzled as it turns in the driveway. "I wasn't expecting anyone," she says, starts for the door. Before she reaches it a man enters. "Scott!" she says. "I didn't know you were back!"

A man in a gray suit takes her in his arms, kisses her. I feel sick, am astonished how much I wanted him not to return. He glances in my direction, they exchange words. She brings him into the living room.

"Ah, Dr. Archer," he says, "how nice to see you again."

"Have we met?"

"But of course. Don't you remember?"

"No . . . though you seem familiar."

"Ah, well. You see so many. I came to your office a long time ago."

I look more closely. Slender, delicate face, gray hair, about thirty-five.

"As a matter of fact, I had been meaning to call you again. Anyway, it's nice to find you here. Why, Ariana, you are blushing! If it were anyone but Dr. Archer I would be jealous."

He slips an arm around her waist, spreads out his hand on her belly. I look at her. She is indeed blushing.

Driving back to the city, I begin to remember him. In my office I look up the record of our meeting. It was ten years ago he had called. "What have you in mind?" I had asked on the phone. "I am acquainted with your work," he had said, as if this were reason enough. When, a few days later, he arrived at my office I found him to be a good-looking man in his twenties with an aura of unusual intensity. His eyes fixed on me, pushed, tried to bore in, take over, eat up. Physically he was light, lithe, wore sandals, slacks, a white shirt, open collar, no tie or jacket, carried a large leather portfolio, a small metal cylinder, and an attaché case. His hand was wet; his clasp was hard, with a tremor.

He sat directly before me, looked at me calmly, waited. I made a gesture as if to say, "Well? . . ." He smiled politely, made pretty much the same gesture. He was going to be difficult. "Tell me," I said, "why you wanted to see me."

"I am an artist."

"What kind?"

"I create in the medium of film."

"You are a photographer?"

After a pause and bit of inner struggle he accepted the designation. "My task," he said, "is the portrayal of interrelatedness. Of all things in the universe."

"And have you," I asked with a glance at the portfolio,

"brought some of your work to show me?" He nodded and took up the metal cylinder which became, as he pulled, a tripod, then to my astonishment something like a music stand. He walked about my office, observing sources and intensities of light, set up the stand about four feet from me, opened his portfolio, and slowly, as if handling thin porcelain, put a mounted photograph on the stand. He then resumed his seat and looked away, as if prepared to wait a long time.

It appeared as a mass of snakes, tangled forms in violent sinister motion, but on closer inspection was seen as a proliferation of roots. It gave a sense of tortured but invincible writhing, struggling, seeking. An astonishing photograph. He showed others—photomicrographs of trichomonads swarming in a vagina, fungus devouring the feet of an athlete, mushrooms sprouting cancerously on rotting logs. Each he would place before me in the same portentous manner, sitting back and turning away to allow me undisturbed communion with his art.

When I said that these were remarkable and original photographs he seemed to relax, became more willing to talk, and related then the story of a sensitive boy growing up as an only child in a wealthy family. He had written poetry, painted, some years ago had dropped out of college, worked with tutors, become more isolated, had written a book called *The Meaning of Form*. He opened the attaché case and took out a manuscript. I glanced through the table of contents, read a few paragraphs. It was almost four hundred pages, the language was swollen, much to do about interrelatedness; some of it was written in the form of poetry; the aim was a comprehensive theory of esthetics. No one would publish it, he said, and no one would publish his pictures. He spoke with contempt of the

"Establishment" from which, however, he seemed bitterly eager for recognition.

He had an injured, mistreated air. Did he regard the frustrations of art as an illness? "Interesting," I said, handing back the manuscript, "but why did you want to see a psychiatrist?"

He could stall no longer. After a pause he sighed heavily. "I am obsessed with sex." He sighed again, and I waited to hear the account of a blocked and twisted drive. "It's always on my mind," he said. "I wake with it in the morning, it's with me through the day, nothing satisfies it. It interferes with my work, is taking over my whole life . . . wanting young women—not any one, but hundreds, endlessly. Shaken by it, torn. When I walk on the street, see a girl, begin undressing her in thought, examine breasts, nipples, spread her behind, look at her pubic hair . . . in great detail, I can't stop it . . . I'll hurry to keep up with her, imagine every little thing. When I go to buy film there's a blonde waits on me, I can't remember what I wanted for looking at her legs, breasts. I go to the bank and there they are, the pretty girls . . . don't even have to be pretty. Even the ugly ones, I look at them the same way. I want to own, explore every one. I open the newspaper and there—it never fails— some picture of a nearly naked girl. If you look at the movie page it's a seething mass of bodies. I pick up the mail, the advertisements, there they are: manuals of sexual technique, encyclopedias of sex, how to have bigger and better orgasms, married love, illustrations, perversions, anything. Any magazine—there they are, the bikinis . . . particularly in my profession . . . any journal on film. . . ."

It was difficult not to smile. He was so petulant, so

53

carried away, so passionate in his sense of injustice.

"It's not that I'm frustrated, not that I'm alone. I'm married, very happy with my wife." This surprised me. "It's not as though she were frigid; she's loving, responsive. We have intercourse every night, sometimes three or four times, sometimes in the morning too. During the day she's always there if I want her. Nothing helps. It's not as though she were unattractive; she's a beautiful woman. Everyone says so.

"I've tried everything. 'Why can't I want only what I have?' I say to myself, 'especially since what I have is the best I could want.' It doesn't work. I try to avoid stimulation . . . weeks when I won't open a newspaper or magazine for fear of those girls in girdles and bras. I denounce my obsession as having nothing to do with love—which it doesn't—nothing in fact to do with girls as human beings. I don't really want any of them, no interest, just a way of loving myself—girl-seeking is self-seeking. . . . It doesn't help.

"I have tried everything," he repeated mournfully, ". . . but infidelity." His eyes were glazed, he turned to the window. "I've never had a woman but Ariana—that's my wife. Never even touched one. Never will. I really love her . . . I'd do nothing to lose it. Sometimes in a strange city, in a hotel room, lying on the bed looking up at the ceiling, the unfamiliar noises, smells . . . I think of asking the bell captain to send a girl, my hand will move to the phone . . . but I stop it, I never would. Not that Ariana would know," he turned back to me, "but *I* would know. That would make the difference.

"Young people now are promiscuous," he continued in glum pedantry, "don't know what love is. Ask them, 'Are you in love?' they get confused, embarrassed, don't know what to say, don't understand the question. 'We get along,' they say. Or 'We pick up a lot of kicks,' or 'We have a good sexual relationship.' No barriers. When desire flows free it never builds up the tension out of which love is made. I really believe that. Love is not a gift but a creation, is made anew by each generation out of something more common. For this to happen the primitive material has to be accumulated. The promiscuous accumulate nothing, wander around like animals discharging indiscriminately, never bring together enough raw material, never subject it to sufficient pressure, to ignite it into love."

His eyes, lighted with fanatic glare, began to push at me again, recruit me for a crusade. "Love is not libido, I write about that," he touched his manuscript: "it's the imposition of form on libido, comes into being only with the energy saved by forcing delay in the discharge of drive."

He was in my bailiwick now, jargon and all, and knew it, was challenging, pressing into me with the points of those eyes. I listened, neither signing up nor turning away, and he lapsed into baffled silence.

"I try to keep this from Ariana," he said gloomily, "but she knows. I see her watching me as I look at her *Vogue* magazine. I turn the pages lightly, affecting the disinterested curiosity of photographer or sociologist. 'These pictures,' I say, 'were taken by men who fear and hate women; these clothes were designed by such men. The whole magazine is a sick collaboration between male homosexuality and female narcissism.' But she knows."

The time had come for a decision. Did I want him? Could I listen to this sort of thing hour after hour? for years? It was pretty thick. He was interesting, intelligent, but there was something I didn't like. He was too hungry.

Nothing would ever fill him. "I do not myself have time," I said; "but you ought to have treatment. If you wish I will refer you."

He sighed, began returning the photographs to his portfolio. His face reproached me, his expression became suspicious, hostile. "Why did you let me talk, why lead me on," he seemed to be thinking, "if you weren't going to take me?" This was just what I didn't like about him, this thinking himself as so special, deserving, wanting the advantages of conflict without the stress. "It shouldn't happen to me!" he was saying; "it shouldn't be so hard!" And there was something else, something I couldn't put my finger on.

As he was closing the attaché case his hands trembled violently, he looked up with boyish fear, helplessness. I was touched, about to say something, but he recovered immediately, settled back. Apparently he was not ready to go. His expression became secret, cunning.

"I had very much hoped," he said, "to be treated by you. I have read your work, know something of your thought, respect you. . . . Perhaps if I waited a few weeks? . . ." I shook my head.

"Money is not the main consideration," he said reflectively, as if thinking aloud. "My grandmother left a trust. What's really important is to get over this obsession. So . . . any fee would be all right . . . any hour, evenings, Saturday? . . ." I shook my head.

He stood up, prepared to leave, paused. He had one more gambit.

"Most of my work," he said casually, "has been with flora. However, I have done a few studies of the human form, using my wife as model." He took from his case a group of photographs bound as a book. "Would you care to see?" He did not offer it exactly, but slightly extended his hand, an alert, questioning look on his face. If I wanted his wife I would have to reach. I reached.

The book consisted of twelve photographs without captions mounted on white board, held together in a spiral binder, titled in hand lettering *The Rendezvous*. The first photograph, taken from within a house looking out, showed a young woman in silk print dress, high heels, carrying a handbag, no hat. She was running up a cobbled path, waving, smiling. The second was a close-up of her face, mouth shaped for a kiss. The third, within the house, showed her pulling her dress over her head, back arched forward. In the fourth, sitting on the bed in bra and panties, she peels a stocking from upstretched leg. Next she is naked, seen from behind as she walks toward the bathroom. Then in a tub, soapsuds about her shoulders, black hair pinned up, slender neck, one leg above the water, small ankle. Then in profile, standing, beginning to dry herself, apples of heaven. The sequence teased, but was honest: in the last but one she is full front, no towel, arms to her sides, the completely naked woman, every pubic hair defined. The last photograph was darker, the camera supine: hair falling across her face, she enters the bed.

My heartbeat shook me, throat constricted. She was about twenty. . . . I flipped through quickly, looked up to find a faint smile on his face. He had relaxed, seemed to imply I might perhaps find time after all. "Excellent photographs," I said drily and dismissed him, again offering to arrange for his treatment by another psychiatrist.

I suffer a bit myself from the ailment of which he complained, and for days was haunted by that girl. She had a lyrical quality which transcended, I thought, his photographic intentions, even his comprehension. The design was lascivious, but he had been unable to make her dirty. That was the remarkable thing: while commanding her physical compliance her spirit had escaped him—and he hadn't noticed. I was most insistently visited by that last picture but one, her coming toward the camera, uncovered, defenseless, black hair falling over her shoulders, on her face an inwardness of look—and could imagine the rest: the darkened room, husband bending over the tripod, peering through the view finder, zeroing in on her pubis. Naked before the lens, unable to hide from herself the shabbiness of her husband's character, she yet retained a dignity that made my heart leap in admiration.

I thought of her as captive, wanted to rescue her, considered calling him, taking him on after all—not for his sake but hers, indirectly to make life better for her. For how could she be other than miserable with this man? Several times during the following weeks I drove by the address he had given me. From the first photograph I recognized the pine tree and the cobbled path to the front door. I was hoping to see her entering or leaving.

It was all nonsense, of course, and gradually I forgot it, took some comfort from the thought that though he might exploit her there was something wonderful and elusive about her he would never command because he could not perceive.

VI

The next day I telephone. "Oh, hello, Doctor," Scott says.
"How nice to hear from you again so soon." "May I speak
to Ariana?" "But of course," he says with an inflection that
takes my question literally. There is a long wait before I
hear her voice. "Hello? . . . Hello? . . ." She sounds far
away, faint, preoccupied. I struggle to reach her. "May I
see you today?" "I think . . . better not." I can barely
hear her. "When?" I shout. "We are busy. Perhaps . . .
later . . . next week." I call two days later; Emily answers,
comes back to say, "She's not in." Three days later I call
in the morning. The phone rings many times. "Hello." It is
Ariana. "I must see you. When can I come?" "Now."

I cancel my appointments, go immediately; leave my car
in the driveway, am starting toward the studio when the
front door opens and she calls. I am terribly happy, run to
meet her, put out my hand. "You're not working?" "No."
She wears a white silk blouse with long sleeves, a full skirt
of gray flannel, brown shoes, white socks.

She takes me in the living room, invites me with a
gesture to sit. She stands, wanders about, picks up small
objects from the brick ledge over the fireplace—a brass
rabbit, a jade dish, an Indian fetish—dusts them with her
fingers, wipes the dust on the other hand. Her mouth
twitches, vertical wrinkles appear on her forehead.

"Where is Scott?"

She shrugs. "Away . . . working."

She drops the jade dish, which breaks, picks up the
pieces, for a moment tries to fit them together, tosses them
on the mantel.

"More precisely," she says suddenly, "he is in Baja, California. A skindiver discovered an underwater grotto which serves as a brothel for dolphins." She speaks harshly, looks directly at me. "Believe that or not, as you like. Anyway, constant and promiscuous sexual intercourse among dolphins is said to occur there. Scott"—she looks at her watch—"is in a diving bell sixty-five feet underwater photographing the action." She shrugs again. "Let's walk."

We go through the woods above her studio, climb the hill to the cemetery. The graves are Spanish from the first half of the nineteenth century. Once there was a mission and churchyard, now overgrown with grass. We sit on a low wall of stone, once a foundation.

"He was born with a blueprint for life," she says, "can't find any reality to fit it."

"Strange . . ." I say, "during the past days I've been thinking of him so enviously."

She frowns, shakes her head. "Will you help him?"

"I don't want to treat him. I'm in love with you."

She stands up. "Don't be," she says briefly. "I want a friend."

"I can't help it." I take her shoulders, her blouse comes open, there are bruises on her neck. "What's this?"

She shakes her head, walks on. We come to a meadow; she picks orange poppies, lilac and columbine, becomes excited, bends quickly, jerks at the flowers. I catch her, take her arm. "What a mood you're in!"

There are tears in her eyes. She throws the flowers in the air, they fall on my head, shoulders. She laughs, arranges them in my hair, over my ears; suddenly stops. "I do like you very much," she says, takes my hand.

Presently we come to the top of a rise. Below us is a steep slope, a barbed-wire fence, a plowed field. Two dogs are stuck together, stand awkwardly in the black earth, move slowly. The male is a large German shepherd with unusual markings—white with black nose, black ears, and black tail—the bitch is a sleek gray mongrel, much smaller. They rotate painfully, tugging slightly. The male is the more uncomfortable, snarls at the bitch. I put my hand on Ariana's arm, she removes it irritably. Four children appear below to our left, stand at the barbed wire, begin to hoot and jeer. They climb through the fence, surround the dogs, throw clods of fresh earth. The dogs helplessly endure the insult, the German shepherd snarls, snaps.

I put my arm around Ariana, feel tension in her waist. Abruptly she starts back, walks fast, we do not speak. When we enter the house I take her arm. "Now, what's the matter? Tell me." I touch her bruised neck. "What happened?"

For a moment she looks in my face, then puts her head on my shoulder. I try to kiss her, but she avoids my lips. I find something in her touch, in her dark hair, I will not forget. Her arms go around me, she holds me tightly, then stands back.

"Now you must go, my dear," she says, "and not come back. Not for a long time. Not till you get over this."

I begin to object, but see a look of pain. She is weary, pleading.

The following days when I telephone, Emily asks who is calling, tells me Mrs. Craig is not in. The next week it is Scott who answers. "Oh, hello, Doctor. How nice of you to keep in touch." "May I speak to Ariana?" "But of course," he says, but after a minute returns to say, "Sorry, old chap, she's all tied up."

My phone rings at three in the morning. I struggle up from sleep. "Max?" It's Ariana. A wave of desire lifts me

awake. "I'm worried about Scott." "What? . . ."
"Shaking . . . thinks he's dying. I can't calm him, have
nothing. . . ." "I'll come." "No, don't, but have something
sent." "I'll come." "But . . ." "There's no drugstore open,"
I say, "and who could ever find you?" And I want to see
you, I think, am obliged to Scott.

It's a black night, the highway is deserted. I pass the last
streetlight in San Anselmo, enter the forest of redwood,
from a distance see the lighted house. Ariana meets me at
the door, hair loose, wears a blue wood housecoat to her
ankles, takes my hand, leads me upstairs to a large square
room with low ceiling, white walls, walnut shutters, dark
oak plank floor, two chests, not much furniture. Scott
cowers on a large bed. Unable to decide whether to face
danger or cover his head, he arrives at a cramped
compromise—half sitting, half lying, twisted on his side,
sheet held tight around his face like a girl at the approach
of a rapist. I stand beside the bed. "Hello, Scott," extend
my hand, wait, until finally from under the sheet he
extracts his own, wet and trembling.

"Let me talk to him alone," I say to Ariana. She brings
me a chair. I hear her footsteps down the stairs, ankles
crossing, recrossing.

"Now, Scott, what's the matter?" "I don't know." "What
do you feel?" "Afraid." "Of what?" "I don't know.
Nothing."

He whispers, his pulse is 120, his temperature seems
normal.

"When did this start?" "I was falling asleep." "How did
you spend the evening?" "Reading a magazine." "And
Ariana?" "Drawing." "When to bed?" "Eleven." "Both of
you?" "Yes." "Were you all right then?" "Yes." "What did
you talk about?" "Nothing." "Sexual relations?" "Yes."

"Anything unusual?" "No." "Then what happened?" "Had almost fallen asleep . . . began to shake."

I ask more questions, learn nothing. He becomes less frightened as we talk. I give him three grains of barbiturate. "Now you will sleep," I tell him. "Lie still. Close your eyes. In a few minutes you will be asleep."

Ariana is waiting at the foot of the stairs. "What do you think?" she asks.

"I don't know. Anything unusual today?"

"No."

"I'll see him this afternoon. Maybe he can tell me more."

She lays her hand on my arm. I want her like this, wanting something of me, but for herself. "What have you noticed?" I ask.

"Sometimes . . . a sort of cruelty. He was always so gentle."

"How, cruel?"

"I don't know. Nothing . . . definite." I know she's lying. "Something I feel . . . I may be wrong. An intuition."

"Anything unusual in bed tonight?"

She blushes. "No."

"Did he hurt you?"

"No."

Under the blue robe she wears a lavender silk nightgown, lace at throat and ankles. "I'm going now," I say curtly.

"Will you help him?"

I look at her mouth, drawn with anxiety, am jealous of her concern. "I'm in love with you," I say angrily.

"Oh, my dear . . ."

Upstairs a door opens, bare feet running. Scott peers

down the stairs. "Ariana! Doctor. Come stay with me."

"I'm leaving now," I tell him. "You go back to bed. Lie still. In a few minutes you will sleep."

Reluctantly he returns to the bedroom.

"Don't love me," Ariana says, standing close. "I'm not free, don't want you to be unhappy. But . . . if you care for me I'd be grateful if you help him."

It is a different man who appears at my office twelve hours later. Casually dressed in loafers, slacks, tweed jacket, manner easy and relaxed, ready smile, firm dry handshake. "So good of you to come last night," he says. "It's few doctors who'll do that, you know. I'm honored as well as indebted. And you did cure me. I went right to sleep, no dreams, didn't wake till noon. Now it's all over. I'm fine."

"I didn't cure you," I say. "And you're not fine. Whatever was wrong last night is still wrong, just not hurting."

He laughs. "How blunt you are!"

"So . . . what was ailing you?"

"I've been thinking about it all the way here. I simply don't know. It was a perfectly calm and ordinary day, beginning to end."

I watch him, wait. He meets and returns my gaze; after a few moments turns up his hands, smiles. "Really . . . I have no idea."

"I don't believe you."

A pause. He shrugs. "Nevertheless . . ."

"You could not be so unaware," I say, "must have some clue . . . intimation." He becomes thoughtful, reviews the day. A minute passes. "What comes to mind?"

"Last night after we made love Ariana was lying very still. She . . ." He breaks off, gives me an appraising glance. "It had been a romp. The covers were off, pillows on the floor, the bed a platform covered with a sheet. I stood up, looked at her. She was naked"—I feel anger rising—"lying on her back, absolutely still . . . face turned away from me. Her arms were spread out, legs open. She looked . . . it's hard to explain. She looked heavy—because she was relaxed, I suppose, like a dead weight. But she made no impression . . . on the bed, I mean . . . didn't sink in." He makes a puzzled gesture, shakes his head. "Nothing mysterious. I don't know why I mention it. It's a hard bed."

He stops, presently seems to have given up this train of thought. "Go on," I say.

He turns his eyes on me with a blank stare. "I stood there looking at her. She didn't move. Something disturbed me, and I knew what it was like . . . as if she had fallen from a height." He shrugs, smiles. "Is that a clue?"

"Perhaps. Go on."

"Nothing. If there was anything else I missed it."

"Did you ever have the treatment I recommended ten years ago?"

"No."

"You need it pretty bad," I say. "Last night should be a warning."

"I like to talk to you. Perhaps we . . ."

"It would not be me." He seems disappointed. "What happened to your obsession?"

"Ah, you remember that! What an ass I was. You must have been very amused."

"I was not."

"You're kind. Well, the obsession . . . I don't know. Perhaps I still have it, but it doesn't bother me any more."

"Why?"

"Because"—he grins impishly—"now I act it out."

"How did that come about?"

"Bones. Human bones. Thousands and thousands of skeletons."

He waits for a reaction but seems content presently to continue without it. "Have you heard of the Well of Osiris? . . . no? The greatest anthropological find since Sumer. In Uganda, high up in the Ruwenzori Mountains, west of Lake Victoria. Strange place. Dense fogs hang motionless for days over bottomless crevasses; giant orchids three feet across turn slowly, watch as you pass. . . . No, really. Thermotropism—if jargon helps you. The botanists say they are supersensitive to heat, pick up radiation from a human body, fix on it, follow like"—his eyes gleam to an inner vision—"a beautiful, loving . . . sinister radar. They're deep purple, some of them almost black; they turn to watch you, wait for you to come back, they have . . . intentions. And sometimes, suddenly, out of that gray flannel fog, that heavy silence, a huge orange bird flies by, so close you fall down to miss the brilliant wing, and just for a moment you look up and see a green eye fixed on you. The stare has meaning, the encounter was planned. The eye is perfectly round, has no depth, no mercy. The bird screams—you could hear it a mile—disappears in the fog. You can't see anything then, can't hear any wings, it never happened, but you *know* it happened.

"Great flood there a few years ago. A huge cliff was undermined, fell sheer away into an abyss, exposed a honeycomb of caves going down hundreds of feet, going back in time fifty thousand years, filled with human bones, weapons, jewelry, tools, drawings on the walls, predynastic hieroglyphics.

"I went there as a photographer with the Harvard

expedition, about fifteen of us, including three female graduate students. Ariana stayed in Cambridge. Everything had to be photographed before it was moved, all the artifacts, all the bones. Most of all we worked with bones, Lucy and I. I would photograph them, she would label them, and together we would box them. She was twenty-three, very bright, Radcliffe graduate, round face, brown hair, shining apple cheeks; squeezed her plump bottom into what must have been her little brother's jeans, wore a faded blue shirt with one button missing. In the six months we were there she never sewed on that button. She was married, husband at the Sorbonne studying French literature. Charming wholesome girl, we got along fine.

"Many of the skeletons were intact, every bone in place, rings on the fingers, rings which once had pierced ears and nose and lips, now fallen by the fleshless skulls; iron castration rings now fallen back in the empty, lustless pelves. They were so dead, so long and utterly dead. A flicker of life they had had, eons ago, and the more we learned of the way they had lived the clearer it became they had wasted even that. Those castration rings, for example, the first-born male of every woman—into the ring with the little penis until it swells, becomes gangrenous, falls off. You could see the whole sequence in the wall drawings. Everything we learned about them was some fantastic superstition, taboo. They hunted the giant carnivorous genet, spotted like a leopard and very dangerous, and they had good weapons—spears, shields, iron swords—but a boy went on his first hunt unarmed and alone, to prove his manhood. In one culture all the pretty girls were sacrificed to the gods. Can you imagine? At sixteen, as virgins, they were burned alive on a huge altar of white stone in batches of ten; only the ugly were spared. So the people became uglier and uglier, with small twisted bones, finally disappeared altogether. In another culture we found a religion that barred men from sexual relations with women until their mothers had died; so the young men were homosexual, fathers were aged, and matricide was the crime of passion. And so it went. Wherever the drawings and hieroglyphics could be understood, there would be another fantastic prohibition, some life-destroying leech of sacred convention fastened on the backs of those poor bastards. Always in the name of what they held most holy. For hallowed myths they shortened their already short lives, made them more painful, drier. Anything juicy or fun, like those virgins—that was for the gods.

"Life is particularly short in that part of the world. A child puts his hand on a black liana, discovers too late it's a mamba; in twenty minutes he's dead. At night we would see fires in the mountains, hear the drums of the Bakonjo, sometimes they attacked the village, killed the children, and twice their spears ripped through our tents at night while they howled and screeched in the woods. Sometimes we caught glimpses of them—tiny little men, three feet high, shrunken, wrinkled bodies painted chalk white, teeth filed to points. They're on their way out, have deformed themselves to the edge of extinction, soon will be as much an archeological memory as any other of those vanished cultures.

"The longer I worked there the shorter became life, the longer became death, and the lesson of those bones began to seep in. Since we found no culture in which life was not diminished by taboo, this must be true of all cultures. Have you ever studied the Battle of the Somme? The English advanced upright in a straight line, an arm's length

apart, at a steady walk, with sixty-six pounds of equipment—against machine-gun fire. Because they were so
ordered by an officer representing the crown. Thirty
thousand died the first day. Moral behavior . . . to have
acted otherwise would have been treason. It's not so
different. How can we claim a better basis for what we
hold sacred than could those pre-Egyptians?

"And what about me personally? What hidden tax was
levied on my life? I thought of some successor of mine fifty
thousand years hence, photographing my bones,
reconstructing the way I had lived. How was I now,
unnoticed, wasting my life that would move him then to
pity?

"Well, it was obvious. I had no more than to ask. Here I
was eight thousand miles from home burning up with
wanting Lucy, and she seemed the willing sort, and I did
nothing. Obligation, loyalty, some notion that love,
whatever that is, requires fidelity—considerations which one
day would seem as absurd, if they could be reconstructed
at all, as any restriction suffered by the people whose
bones lay before me. My successor, indeed, might never
have heard of monogamous marriage or romantic love. 'We
cannot account for their behavior,' he might have to say,
referring to Lucy and me. 'Physically they appear to have
been normal; so we must assume that some primitive
taboo, which they held sacred, required their abstinence.'
And he would feel for me the same rueful pity—which
would do me as little good, would be as much too late—as
I felt for the poor bastards whose bones I was
photographing.

"One afternoon Lucy and I were at our usual work. The
cave was filled with an ancient stillness, a fine white dust
covered our hands and faces. Presently I held a skull

before my face, waggled it at her. She laughed. I picked up a female pelvis, held it before her own which filled out her jeans so roundly, snugly, moved it slightly from side to side. She moved to my motion, took the pelvis herself, began to dance with it. Notebook and pencils and labels were forgotten. I took a pelvis for myself and we danced with each other, gaily, pressing together those ancient empty basins, and within moments were on the ground laughing, straining into each other, her legs up and kicking in the dusty air, lips powdered with death.

"I was thirty-three, had never had a woman but Ariana, felt terrible guilt. It's the way any culture enforces restrictions. My existence had lost its authorization. I was determined to find another, to become my own authority, to live close to the gut and to the earth. 'I am what I do,' I told myself angrily, 'I will do as I want to be, and I want to be a guiltless man, a man who, were he able to look back over a span of cosmic time at his flicker of life, would find nothing to regret, would say, "I did that well, as full and rich as possible." I want to live *sub specie aeternitatis*.' I worked hard at it. Every day Lucy and I made love among the bones."

I look at my clock, have had enough of this. He pulls at something in me. I don't want my sympathy engaged. "You need treatment, Scott. I will refer you."

"Why not you?"

"I've become a friend to your wife."

"So we're just where we were ten years ago," he says, smiling. "Strange, you know, I was not at all sure I wanted to come here, but now that I have I want to go on. But not with just anyone. Someone who understands the sickness of just breathing . . . and you do. That's why I put so much stock in its being you." He pauses, questioning. I shake my head. "I really mean it," he says. "I don't want treatment. It's life that ails me, not illness. I just want to talk to you . . . in a way that should not be precluded by friendship, but rather made easier. Might that be possible? Could we meet socially? My wife would be delighted. She speaks of you so . . . fondly."

We are, indeed, just where we were ten years ago: I am refusing him treatment and he is offering me his wife. This time I am less wise. "Sure. Why not?"

VII

A few days later Ariana invites me to a picnic. They are ready when I arrive at eleven, the station wagon packed with blankets, beach chairs, a large wicker hamper. Scott drives us through the coastal hills to the ocean, where we find an isolated spot among the dunes, settle ourselves for lunch. The day is overcast with heavy black clouds in the distance. The yellow sea grass on the dunes stirs slightly in a warm wind. No smell of rain, yet a strangely dark day.

The basket contains a shaker of martinis, pheasant, smoked turkey, red wine, coffee, pastry, candy. Ariana serves from a small folding table set with tablecloth and silver; we eat and drink in a remarkable, though not uncomfortable, silence. Ariana wears a tweed skirt and a yellow silk blouse, unusually vivid against the dark sky and leaden sea. Her loose black hair moves slightly in the warm wind. She appears calm, without need to talk; Scott seems lost in reverie; I wait.

When we have finished eating, Scott says, "Since talking in your office I have come upon what may be another clue. Shall I tell you?" I glance at Ariana, who is repacking the hamper, no help. "I don't want to impose a busman's holiday," Scott says, "but as you were so kind to see me . . . I feel I should share with you whatever turns up."

Ariana still does not meet my gaze. "As you like," I say.

"It lies in my African venture," Scott says. "Every day, as I told you, Lucy and I would make love among the bones. We couldn't use her tent because of Liz and Erica, but after a week or two Erica found out anyway, didn't say anything, but was disturbed, excited. It seemed unfair to her, I think, that Lucy, who was married, should have me while she, who was single, had no one. She became ostentatious in contempt, alluded to our absent spouses, and presently I began to want her too, just for the hell of it. I knew Lucy would be angry, but why, I asked myself— having deferred neither to the imagined hurt to my wife nor to my own guilt feelings—should I defer to that? I found no good reason, so took Erica one morning by the river while she was washing clothes. She was pretty dull, and once was all of her I wanted. For a week or two she waited for more, would leave camp on solitary walks with a parting glance at me. When it became clear I was through, she grew distant, icy, and by the time she returned to Urbana, Illinois, had created the illusion that *she* had rejected me.

"Liz was a different sort. A tiny thing like a child, twenty-two but only four feet ten, weighed ninety pounds, slender little bones; quiet, self-contained, very serious— much like Ariana—doing her dissertation in philology, something about hieroglyphics, worked late every night. I put my arm around her; she removed it. I kissed her; she said no. Kissed her again; she slapped me. She had no conflict, just didn't want me, and—can you believe it? so vain I had become on two conquests!—it hurt my feelings. I brooded, watched her, wanted her more. And why, I began to ask myself, having deferred to nothing else, should I defer to her no?

"One day . . ."

Ariana stands. "I'm going for a walk."

"No, stay," Scott says, taking her arm. "I can talk about these things so much better with you here." For a long moment they look at each other; the pull on her arm increases. She sits beside him. He strokes her hair, absently runs his fingers over the yellow blouse.

"One day I was driving Liz to another excavation site some miles away. It was midday and hot. We came to a shallow stream to be forded. I stopped the jeep midstream, began to kiss her. She struggled, broke away, I jumped out, caught her. She said 'No! No!' began to fight. She hit me in the face, I pinned her arms. She began to kick, we fell together. The water was a few inches deep swirling over large round rocks, we rolled over and over. She was kicking, was bruised on the rocks. She bit my neck, broke loose, struggled to the bank. I caught her again. She was still kicking but weaker, and again we fell. It was harder now for her to roll and twist; I lay on her, let my weight subdue her. We were lying in dry red dirt and soon were covered, it streamed from our faces like blood. She wore a khaki skirt matted up around her tiny waist; white cotton panties now torn, red with mud. As she grew weaker I pushed at these panties, finally tore through. On and on we fought, gasping, coughing for breath—who would ever have thought such a child's body would have such stamina! An endless ordeal, a committed contest, a kind of marriage. The sun beat down, the red sweat blinded us. Finally I forced her legs open, got in, and still she struggled, but so weak I had only to avoid her teeth.

"I looked up then and saw a huge black man by the stream. He wore a red loincloth, carried a tall spear. I'd never seen such a man. A Zulu, I think. I don't know why, but I wasn't afraid. Somehow I knew he wouldn't attack. He simply stood there, watched, and I watched him while I moved slowly in Liz. When she felt me start to come, she made her last effort to throw me off, a feeble convulsion, the most delicious of all movements, then it was over. We were exhausted, gasping hoarsely, neither of us could move. The black man had gone, I never saw him again. Finally I was able to stand up. She lay there on her back in the dirt, motionless, legs apart, arms stretched out, like a dying starfish, face turned away—remember? just like Ariana on the bed the other night? Is that a clue?"

He falls silent, doesn't want an answer. I watch him, wait. Ariana is still.

"I dipped my shirt in the stream, began to clean her face. I got her to her feet, led her into the water, washed her legs, arms, combed her hair. She did not resist. I lifted her into the jeep and we drove back without speaking. I reported an accident, said we were shaken up, nothing serious—took her to her tent. She disappeared inside, still without a word, closed the flap.

"In my own tent I lay on my cot looking up at the green canvas, thought 'Now I have gone too far.' I remembered the journey to this place—Mombasa, where we disembarked, the long railroad trip to Kampala. There we had become a caravan of jeeps and trucks, traveled slowly, often there were no roads. We crossed a strange high plateau, and day after day was like this one, skies overcast, dark, ominous. The land grew wilder, the trees gaunt, leafless . . . branches frozen in anguished gesticulation. The animals became strange, the natives savage, menacing. We were going back, literally, to the beginning of time, and I felt something sinister lying ahead, waiting. 'Now I know,' I thought, lying there on the cot. 'This is it. I have gone back not as a visitor as I had thought, but an actor, have become a savage, and any moment now the chief of our expedition with two native policemen will enter the tent, arrest me. I will be taken to Nairobi for trial before an English judge in a white wig, then to jail. This is the end to which logic has brought me.'

"But nothing happened. After a while I began to shake and sweat . . . like the other night. Lucy came into the tent. 'What the hell happened to you?' she said, then was overcome with sympathy, began kissing me, called the doctor, thought I had malaria. Nothing ever happened. Liz never said a word to anyone—why, I can't imagine. Perhaps you've heard there's no such thing as rape, that forcible entry is lubricated by covert compliance. I know better. Liz fought to her utmost, held nothing back. Maybe that's why she didn't report me, didn't need to: nothing corrupt in her that needed hiding by the exposing of corruption in me. She has an integrity that must be very rare, that no one else can ever know of her so well as I. Thereafter she held herself at a distance, unapproachable, did not speak. I treated her accordingly, never touched her again, went back to Lucy, with whom I was well content for the rest of our stay."

The warm wind moves aimlessly in the sea grass around us, lifts a strand of Ariana's hair. The tide is coming in, the surf is louder.

"I wonder if you recognize, *Doctor*"—he gives emphasis to the title, puts his hand on my arm—"the terrible thing in this story. Not the rape, but that nothing happened. Can evil which proves so trite remain evil? Must it not disappear altogether in its own banality? No one notices the fall of a sparrow, or the fall of Liz on those rocks. No one cares. It's as simple as that. And when I came back here and told Ariana—after seven years of scrupulous, agonizing fidelity. . . ." He turns up both palms. "Whatdya think? Go ahead. Guess. . . . Nothing happened. You see how unaffected she is? Look!"

I do look. She returns my gaze without embarrassment, an intimate contact of eyes.

"Of course she's heard this before," Scott goes on, "so you may think she is inured? Not so. I'll tell you something now she has *not* heard. This happened yesterday . . . just before noon. I was dictating a letter to my secretary, Edith. She's thirty-five, divorced, warmhearted, an easy lay, I think. Not pretty, has thick legs, small eyes close together. Not my type at all. But one redeeming feature, a beautiful mouth—wide, full. I've done a short motion picture of just her mouth—lips, teeth, tongue, in various conditions: eating, laughing, talking, kissing, smoking, sucking, biting, snoring—must show it to you sometime. It's absolutely pure, nothing pornographic—you could bring your mother— but incredibly exciting. Well anyway, I watched Edith's mouth as I composed the letter—which was a note to a publisher about my fee for the use of photographs. When I had finished she stood up. I swiveled to the side. 'Edith,' I said. She raised her eyes. I uncrossed my legs, slid down an inch in the chair. That's all it took. She . . ." I make an involuntary movement, something rises in my throat. Scott pauses, watches with amusement. " . . . put the blue cap on her ballpoint pen, put pen and pad on the desk—she's the soul of neatness—knelt before me, elbows on my knees . . . the beautiful mouth worked perfectly."

Ariana is looking out to sea, does not move, a dark inwardness of gaze.

"Sweet girl, Edith," Scott continues. "She received my little gift as if with gratitude, stood up, smiled—I felt sorry for her then with those thick ankles—picked up her pad and pencil and left."

He takes a deep breath, sighs. "You see, Ariana accepts these things. They don't hurt her . . . watch out, Doctor, or you'll find yourself wanting to save her from me. You'd be playing the fool."

I've had enough of this. "Since you've made a therapy hour out of this picnic," I say, "I'll give you an interpretation."

"Oh, good!"

"Nothing you've said was intended as exploration of your anxiety attack. You meant only to humiliate your wife—and me, since you know I'm fond of her."

"Excellent," Scott says, raising his hand, touching thumb to forefinger. "Perceptive. Well put."

"What you don't know," I continue, "is that your cruelty is driven. You think you play with it, stop it when you want. But you can't. This is the interpretation: you're compelled, you have no freedom, will destroy yourself. This is why you have to have treatment."

"Hmm. I'll think about that," Scott says, and grins. "But in the meantime, Doctor, I'll give *you* an interpretation. Okay? Brace yourself? You refused me as a patient— accepted me as a friend—only because you want my wife. Right?"

"Yes."

"Marvelous!" Scott breathes. "Marvelous! You tell the truth." Then laughs loudly. "Now, Doctor, what about Ariana? We've exposed a bit of dirt in each other, what shall we say of her? Is she lily white? Tell us, sweetheart. You're among friends. Strictest confidence and all that." Ariana, unsmiling, looks at him, shakes her head. "Ah, resistance! Resistance! She won't talk, Doctor. Some kind of basic mistrust. I'll say it for her: She would have us think she invited you because I suggested it. She uses my need for therapy to hide her wish to be with you. Look—pay dirt—she blushes! You've made a conquest, Doctor. Congratulations!"

Ariana is turned away from us looking out to sea. How odd, I think, that she should blush to this, having held such composure at all the rest. The scalpel hurts more than the ax. I watch as the curved eyelashes are lowered, the color subsides from her cheek. The three of us sit in silence, motionless, a tableau of Sunday Picnic. Scott looks at his feet, seems at the end of his game. Ariana is removed from both of us. Presently I, too, turn away, look at the leaden sea, the pounding surf, the dark beach. The warm wind is still blowing.

"That's the astonishing thing," Scott says. "After we've lived for a while we sum up lost illusions and realize, with a certain despair, that nothing matters. We accept it—it's the way things are—but deep down, unknown to us, we disavow it. Under the façade of nihilism we know that Santa Claus will come, the Angel of God will look after us, all the while saying in our grown-up way, 'Nothing matters.' That's where things stand, that's where we live, most of us, till we die. But if perchance we test it out— hoping, unconsciously, to prove it false—we find it's true. That's the astonishing thing. It's really true. Nothing *does* matter. Then we're broken. Not despair—the worldly pose is lost—but confused . . . terribly."

We sit for a while longer. The picnic box has been repacked. There is nothing to do, nothing more to say. The sky grows darker, the wind increases. Sand begins to bite at our faces.

"Let's go," I say, and we stand, slowly, painfully—put an end to the unhappiest picnic of my life.

When we get to the Craigs' house Scott disappears upstairs without a word. Now it is raining, has suddenly become cold. I am putting on my coat in the hallway. Ariana stands before me, wraps her scarf around my neck, buttons my coat. "Thank you for listening to him," she says. She pulls my face down, kisses my cheek.

"Oh, I'm a listener, all right," I say gloomily.

Friday night comes and I want a woman, examine the list. The names weary me. They try so hard, with such hunger, are driven to such aching search. I see their faces, know their nervousness, the attempts to be sexy, the terrible clichés, the talk of "relationships." Any one I might call would make some muted protest, imply that other men are interested, she doesn't sit by the phone, it's rare for her to be free of a Friday evening; then, having so established the impropriety of my late call, would forgive me, by chance she *is* free, would love to see me. "Give me an hour," she would say, and then would dress so well, be so sparkling, vital, when I arrive—"Darling!" the chilled martinis, "See. I remembered your twist of lemon peel!"— the smart talk over dinner, so knowledgeable at the theater, pulling off the long black gloves, commenting on the preoccupations of the younger playwrights, so well acquainted during intermission, nodding to friends— somehow making me both witness and battleground for her gallant fight against loneliness, the fear of being unwanted; and in bed finally, so serious, so tender, the whispers about "genuine intimacy." I drop the list.

In North Beach I drift past the orifices of blaring music, have a drink at Enrico's. A pack of tourists from Omaha with large white lapel buttons line up inside a Gray Line bus, stumble off shy and dazed, line up again for Finocchio's. Nearby a lady in diamonds and mink with a bored husband is watching me. Her neck is wrinkled, the hunger of age is in her eyes. Too late, baby, too late. I'm not wanting shabby bodies in beautiful clothes, but vice versa, vice versa. I watch the hippies in short skirts, black stockings, loose flying hair. What I want—it's simple: the youngest and prettiest of these girls to love me, that's all. Though herself only twenty she must appreciate all my complexities, hidden recesses of spirit, vulnerabilities of talent; be so drawn to what she finds that flesh will fire, fuse with me, grapple, entangle, become my substance—but no demands; after such a night of creative passion to vanish without a trace, not a question, not even my name. That's all. Any candidates? Step right up, ladies.

I venture a smile at a pretty girl, and get a blank stare which tells me, like a fortune, my age. Maybe too late for me too. In a topless club I watch the tease and the jiggling breasts, have two drinks, cannot bring myself to settle for the old pro who winks from the bar; go on to Port Said, the dive of a belly dancer: phony fakir sitting at the door on artificial nails, pretending to play a pipe before a basket from which a foam rubber cobra sways to canned Turkish music, artificial tongue darting in and out; enter an airless cavern of smoke, a weird complaining din of plucked strings, a stench of packed bodies, and the old smell of burnt fat which clings to the walls; completely dark except for one variably colored spotlight which plays over a nearly naked girl. I sit near the dais, have another drink, watch the writhing arms, the sinuous hips, the mobile belly— would she take me in tonight? She has dark skin, a sultry pouting face. I stare with admiring invitation; her face returns the stare, blank, uncomprehending, while her body continues to express the most perfect comprehension.

The act ends, the girl disappears, the lights come up. I am about to leave when I hear my name. "There's Max. Hello, Max." Scott, in black tie, is coming toward me, smiling, arm outstretched. Ariana follows. "Isn't she marvelous?" he says in his high delicate voice. "Isn't she spectacular?" I think he means Ariana, who is wrapped in a shimmering sari, aquamarine with small rearing horses embroidered in gold; gold slippers, large gold rings in her ears. But he means, rather, the dancer. "She's one of my models," he says. "I did a short movie of her, just the navel."

We shake hands. Ariana smiles warmly, eyes and black hair glisten in the lurid light, takes my hand affectionately.

"An unusual film," Scott goes on. "I'd like to show you. May we join you? . . . Thanks. Has something in common with the one of Edith's mouth I told you about. But this one is more spectacular. Zoë was furious—that's her name, the dancer—because I didn't show her face. At no time. Not even her full figure—just the belly. But that's enough. The things that belly can do! On and on and on like the voice of a hypnotist, never stops, never lets attention wander, gathers you in, holds you tighter, takes over all preoccupations, drains away the awareness of self, finally absorbs you altogether in its ceaseless movement. And the faces that navel can make—sucking, spitting, biting!—yes, really. Many people have an orgasm just watching. You must see it. Would interest you as a psychoanalyst. I'll arrange it.

"Then"—Scott lowers his voice, holds up his hand for emphasis—"when I have the viewer firmly in thrall, when he sits there before the screen, hunched over, mouth open, eyes glazed, penis painfully swollen—then I show him a vision of life. Gradually the belly becomes translucent. You still see it—I never let him go, the movement never stops— but slowly, through it, you begin to see armies clashing, the blitzkrieg rolls through France again, storms rage, the mushroom cloud rises over Hiroshima, children die of starvation, you see floods, elections, plane crashes, parades,

Buchenwald. Then the vision fades, the belly always moving becomes like life itself—opaque with flesh and lust: this is where we came from, this is the passion that drives us, this is all the meaning there is. What do you think I call it?"

"*The Belly,* no doubt."

"But no! *Through a Glass Darkly.* You slightly miss me, always. But no matter. Let me introduce you." He disappears at the back of the room.

Ariana regards me kindly. I know why she is here: dragged by Scott's bizarre, unslakable appetites. And she knows why I'm here: pushed through the streets by humble ache of testicle. Exposed, I feel diminished, am too embarrassed to make fun of it. I shrug, turn away; she takes my hand as if she understands.

Scott returns with the dancer, who wears now a red wrapper. "This is Zoë." I stand. "I saw how much you liked her dance," Scott says gleefully. "Tell her. She'd be so pleased." Ariana seems to know her, nods. Zoë doesn't smile or speak, offers a limp hand. We sit.

"The camera," Scott goes on gaily, "has two positions in reference to the subject—eighteen inches and four inches. The four-inch shots are brief, used only for climactic moments, treat the navel as orifice, as mouth or eye—some have said as anus too, but that's not my thought. At eighteen inches you see the whole belly, sternum to pubis. Stand up, Zoë."

He positions her before me, unties her wrapper, kneels beside me, cups his hands around my eyes. "Like that," he says. "The camera locks in on it. Go on, Zoë, move!"

The belly begins the sinuous enticement I had watched earlier at a distance. I smell her sweat, perfume.

"There!" Scott cries. "Isn't that stunning? Can you see

that on a wide screen? The same shot for the transparencies. Can you imagine—seeing through that belly to the tanks in action, the bombs falling, the torpedoes hitting the ship, the Kamikaze planes."

"Smashing," I say, and push away his hands.

"No, no," he says, "I'm not through. Let me show you the close-up." He draws Zoë forward, cups my vision again. I see only the navel and a small portion of surrounding belly. "Now show him, Zoë!" Scott exclaims. "Make it spit! . . . all right, make it bite! . . . Good. Now make it suck! . . . Isn't that spectacular! That's when the sailors come . . . right there." He stands, gives Zoë an affectionate slap on the fanny. "Most people," he says, rubbing her belly, "would like to have a face as expressive as this." For a moment he puts his cheek against it. Zoë reties her wrapper, sits down, still having said not one word. "Really a most unusual film," Scott says. "You must see it."

Across the table Ariana smiles in tranquil beauty. I feel a welling up of anger. But why shouldn't she laugh, I think furiously. It's funny enough. They sat here in the dark, saw me blown in through that door by lechery like a leaf in a storm, saw me worship at that shrine of skin. Now Scott has rubbed my nose in it.

Scott and I drink, Ariana has nothing. She seems weightless, without needs, a luminous cloud, untouched by smoke, sweat, the stifling closeness. Presently Zoë leaves the table, the lights grow dim. The wailing music begins. "I must go," I say.

"Oh no," Scott says. "We've just started. It's only eleven. Many more places to go, acts to see. Come with us. You'll make Ariana so happy." He turns to her. "Ask him, sweetheart."

She is motionless, eyes lowered, the blue overhead light extending her lashes into long shadows.

"No," I say, "I can't. Thanks anyway."

"Wait!" Scott leans toward me, raises his hand in simulated confidentiality, speaks in stage whisper. "Zoë is indebted to me. I, certainly, am indebted to you. Do you? . . . Would you want? . . . Shall I see if she's free tonight?"

He is amused, his eyes twinkle. He knows how to exploit an advantage. Presently he turns up his hands, shrugs—as if to remind me that I can hardly be above a hunger without which I would not be here. Again I glance at Ariana, in whose face I find sympathy, and again hate her. "Some other time," I say, glancing at my watch. "I've got a date. Good-bye."

I go home, undress, lie on my bed in darkness, look out to the orange lights of the bridge, watch the dark shadow of a freighter slide through the black water, want to leave this city.

The phone rings. "Are you alone?" The question is a courtesy; she knows I'm alone. "Can I come?"

A few minutes later in dressing gown, with tousled hair, thinking it's too late, our moment has passed, I open the door. Suddenly she is in my arms, an exotic bird, glint and tinkle of gold rings and red lips, a faceted jewel rocketing spears of colored light over the brown and gray apartment. She laughs at my surliness, kisses me, hugs me, presents her softness. My anger ebbs. "And what about Scott?" I say.

"He found someone," she says easily. "I can stay if you want me." She stands close, turns her head on my shoulder, a sweetness of black hair in my face. My hands begin to find the curves and hollows that have filled my mind. She undresses and I remember those pictures, that other rendezvous, the cobbled walk, the pine tree, the darkened room. The body unwrapped from the sari has lost nothing, but through what perversities I think mournfully has it been dragged by that crazy man? In what strange places and what odd positions has he placed you, upside down and sideways and swinging by the heels from what tinkling chandeliers, with what orifices penetrated by what parts for what strange sensation? And what might you be wanting of me, beautiful lady? I've no new tricks for you, I'm sure. You show me. Maybe you've never been had by an analyst? Want a Freudian lay? It's not so different. Want me to see right through you? Shall we use the couch of sorrows?

In bed her lips open to me, arms encircle, firm brown hands on my loins, and I want her but there's a dirge in me and getting sadder. So why are you here? I think, run my fingers through the silky black hair around the delicate ear, the skull so slight and fragile, and what fantasy is going on just under my hand? Were you excited by the belly dancer? Is there a Lesbian orgy under my fingers? Or the thought of some sick business Scott is up to? It can hardly be me. I cut no thrilling figure tonight. For whom am I standing in? Should you not rather be decently nauseated?

She is murmuring something in my ear, hand moving on my back, an opening of thighs, when I sense she is driven by no desire at all, but goodness of heart. My questions miss, and I become not less but more excited to realize she knows the gust that swept me through the streets tonight, and, though not sharing it, feels neither scorn nor amusement, but a wish to give, and I take her happily, with an innocence strange to me.

VIII

Freedom is that range of experience wherein events,
courses of action, attitudes, decisions, accommodations are
seen as elective. It may be more or less, so we need ask
how much we want. In small things we always want
choice. What color to paint the house? Buy an Olds or a
Buick? Go to the Bergman film or the Ozawa concert? It
would be onerous to be constrained here. In deeper matters
we want to be held back. We might choose to live or die,
but prefer *not* to choose, want to believe rather that we
have to live. A kind man does not ponder becoming a
sadist, an honest man does not consider whether to become
a bandit; we prefer to consider such matters settled,
removed from choice and hence from freedom.

In between such minor and major issues lies the middle
ground of decision and action wherein some find freedom
and choice while others find constraint and necessity. One
man sees himself inextricably stuck in a marriage, a career,
in obligations to children, relatives, colleagues, bound to his
way and place of life, unable to change. Another in the
same circumstances finds it possible to resign as judge of
the circuit court, divorce a Philadelphia Main Line wife
after twenty-four years of marriage and three children,
move to Italy, live with an actress, take up painting. If we
forgo the moral condemnation we generally visit upon
those of greater scope and daring than ourselves we are
likely to discover great envy.

Necessity is that range of experience wherein events,
courses of action, attitudes, decisions are seen as

determined by forces outside ourselves which we cannot alter. A bored woman says, "I'd like to take a job, but can't leave home because of the children." With that "can't" she alleges necessity: staying home or leaving home is not open, the decision is imposed, runs counter to her wants; she designates her children's needs as her necessity. Her prerogative to do this is clear, is granted, but it must be noted that nothing external to herself requires this view. Certainly her children's needs do not require it: within the same block other mothers manage somehow with babysitters and so hold jobs. The necessity that constrains her does not constrain them; it is of a different order than that which would derive from locked doors and barred windows.

The realm of necessity, therefore, must comprise two categories: the subjective or arbitrary, and the objective or mandatory. Mandatory necessity—like natural law which cannot be disobeyed—is that which cannot be suspended. It derives from forces, conditions, events which lie beyond the self, not subject to choice, unyielding to will and effort. "I wish I had blue eyes," " . . . wish I were twenty again," " . . . wish I could fly," " . . . wish I lived in the court of the Sun King." Such wishes are irrelevant, choice is inoperative; the necessity impartially constrains. And since it cannot be put aside there's not much arguing about it. "If you jump you will fall—whether or not you choose to fly." There is consensus, we don't dwell on it, we accept.

Arbitrary necessity derives from forces within the personality, but construed to be outside. The force may be either impulse or prohibition: "I didn't want to drink, but couldn't help it." That is to say, the impulse to drink does not lie within the "I." The "I," which is of course the locus of choice, does not "want" to drink, would choose otherwise, but is overwhelmed by alien force. "I want to marry you," a woman says to her lover, "want it more than anything in the world. But I can't divorce my husband. He couldn't take it . . . would break down. He depends on me. It would kill him." Here it is loyalty, caring for another's welfare, which is alleged to lie outside the deciding "I," which therefore cannot choose, cannot do what it "wants," but is held to an alien course. As though she were saying, "I do not here preside over internal conflict, do not listen to contending claims within myself to arrive finally at an anguished, fallible decision, but am coerced by mandates beyond my jurisdiction; I yield to necessity." The issue is not one of conscious versus unconscious. The contending forces are both conscious. The issue is the boundary of the self, the limits of the "I."

Arbitrary necessity, therefore—like man-made law—is that which may be suspended, disobeyed. When dealing with ourselves the constraining force seems inviolable, a solid wall before us, as though we really "can't," have no choice; and if we say so often enough, long enough, and mean it, we may make it so. But when we then look about and observe others doing what we "can't" do we must conclude that the constraining force is not an attribute of the environing world, not the way things are, but a mandate from within ourselves which we, strangely, exclude from the "I."

The lady who "wants" to marry her lover but "can't" divorce her husband might here object. "When I said 'can't,' " she might say, "it was just a way of speaking, a metaphor. It meant that staying with my husband represents duty, not desire, that's all. In a theoretical way I could choose . . . I know that. But it's just theoretical. Because . . . you see, the conflict is so terribly unequal, the considerations that make me stay, that absolutely demand I stay with my husband . . . they're so overwhelmingly strong, there's really no choice. That's all I mean."

We make serious record of her objection. In passing we note with surprise that the inequality of the conflict leads her to conclude there is "really no choice," whereas this same circumstance would have led us to say rather that the choice is easy, one she might arrive at promptly, with the conviction of being right.

It's only a metaphor, she says. In some theoretical way, she says, she is aware of choice. Perhaps. But we have doubt. In any event we must point out that she specifically denies this choice for which she now claims oblique awareness, that she locates the determining duty outside the "I" and its "wants." And we might add that if she continues such metaphorical speech long enough she will eventually convince even herself; her "theoretical" choice will become more and more theoretical until, with no remaining consciousness of option, it will disappear in thin air. She then will have made actual something that may once have been but a metaphor. Nothing guarantees our freedom. Deny it often enough and one day it will be gone, and we'll not know how or when.

Objective necessity is not arguable. My lover dies, I weep, beat my fists on the coffin. Everyone knows what I want; everyone knows that nothing will avail, no prayer, no curse, no desperate effort, nothing, that I shall never get her back. When there is argument about necessity, the alleged constraint is arbitrary, subjective. A house in flames, a trapped child, a restraining neighbor: "You can't go in! It's hopeless." I see it differently: I *can* go in—if I have the nerve. There may be a chance. It's not clear whether the situation permits or proscribes; the difference of opinion indicates that the necessity at issue is arbitrary. My neighbor's statement is more plea than observation; he asks me to perceive that the contemplated action is precluded, to "see" that there is no choice. By so deciding I can make it so. If I agree it is impossible, then—even if mistaken—my having arrived at that judgment will, in a matter of moments, make it true. Our judgments fall within the field of events being judged, so themselves become events, and so alter the field. We survey the course of history and conclude, "Wars are inevitable." The judgment seems detached, as if we observed from a distant galaxy; like all judgments, it may be mistaken. In any event it is not inert, it has consequences, shapes action, moves interest and behavior from, for example, the politics of dissent to the connoisseurship of wine; and so chips off one more fragment of the obstacle to war, thereby makes more likely the war which, when it comes, will vindicate our original judgment and the behavior which issued from it. So we create the necessity which then constrains us, constrains ever more tightly day after day, so vindicating ever more certainly our wisdom in having perceived from the outset we were not free. Finally we are bound hand and foot and may exclaim triumphantly, how right we were!

The areas of necessity and of freedom vary in proportion to each other and in absolute measure. They vary, also, from person to person, and, within the same person, from time to time. Together they comprise the total extent of available experience the range of which is a function of awareness and concern.

Adolescence, traditionally, is the time of greatest freedom, the major choices thereafter being progressively made, settled, and buried, one after another, never to be reopened. These days, however, an exhumation of such issues in later life has become quite common, with a corresponding increase in freedom which makes life again as hazardous as in youth.

Throughout our lives the proportion of necessity to freedom depends upon our tolerance of conflict: the greater our tolerance the more freedom we retain, the less our tolerance the more we jettison; for high among the uses of necessity is relief from tension. What we can't alter we don't have to worry about; so the enlargement of necessity is a measure of economy in psychic housekeeping. The more issues we have closed the fewer we have to fret about. For many of us, for example, the issues of stealing and of homosexuality are so completely buried that we no longer have consciousness of option, and so no longer in these matters have freedom. We may then walk through Tiffany's or go to the ballet without temptation or conflict. For one to whom these are still live issues, the choice depending upon a constantly shifting balance of fallibly estimated rewards of gain or pleasure as against risks of capture or shame, such jaunts may cause great tension.

Tranquillity, however, has risks of its own. As we expand necessity and so relieve ourselves of conflict and responsibility, we are relieved, also, in the same measure, of authority and significance. When there arises then a crisis which does not fall within our limited routine we are frightened, without resources, insignificant.

For some people necessity expands cancerously, every possibility of invention and variation being transformed into inflexible routine until all of freedom is eaten away. The extreme in psychic economy is an existence in which everything occurs by law. Since life means conflict, such a state is living death. When, in the other direction, the area of necessity is too much diminished we become confused, anxious, may be paralyzed by conflict, may reach eventually the extreme of panic.

The more we are threatened, fragile, vulnerable, the more we renounce freedom in favor of an expanding necessity. Observing others then who laugh at risk, who venture on paths from which we have turned back, we feel envy; they are courageous where we are timid. We come close to despising ourselves, but recover quickly, can always take refuge in a hidden determinism. "It's all an illusion," we say; "it looks like their will and daring as against my inhibition and weakness, but that *must* be illusion. Because life is lawful. Nothing happens by chance. Not a single atom veers off course at random. My inhibition is not a failure of nerve. We can't see the forces that mold us, but they are there. The genetic and experiential dice are loaded with factors unknown, unknowable, not of our intending, are thrown in circumstances over which we have no vision or control; we are stuck with the numbers that turn up. Beware the man who claims to be captain of his soul, he's first mate at the very best."

The more we are strong and daring the more we will diminish necessity in favor of an expanding freedom. "We are responsible," we say, "for what we are. We create ourselves. We have done as we have chosen to do, and by so doing have become what we are. If we don't like it, tomorrow is another day, and we may do differently."

Each speaks truly for himself, the one is just so determined, the other is just so free; but each overstates his truth in ascribing his constraint or his liberty to life at large. These truths are partial, do not contend with each other. Each expresses a quality of experience. Which view one chooses to express, to the exclusion of the other, better describes the speaker than the human condition.

In every situation, for every person, there is a realm of freedom and a realm of constraint. One may live in either realm. One must recognize the irresistible forces, the iron fist, the stone wall—must know them for what they are in order not to fall into the sea like Icarus—but, knowing them, one may turn away and live in the realm of one's freedom. A farmer must know the fence which bounds his land, but need not spend his life standing there, looking out, beating his fists on the rails; better he till his soil, think of what to grow, where to plant the fruit trees. However small the area of freedom, attention and devotion may expand it to occupy the whole of life.

Look at the wretched people huddled in line for the gas chambers at Auschwitz. If they do anything other than move on quietly, they will be clubbed down. Where is freedom? . . . But wait. Go back in time, enter the actual event, the very moment: they are thin and weak, and they smell; hear the weary shuffling steps, the anguished catch of breath, the clutch of hand. Enter now the head of one hunched and limping man. The line moves slowly; a few yards ahead begin the steps down. He sees the sign, someone whispers "showers," but he knows what happens here. He is struggling with a choice: to shout "Comrades! They will kill you! Run!" or to say nothing. This option, in the few moments remaining, is his whole life. If he shouts he dies now, painfully; if he moves on silently he dies but minutes later. Looking back on him in time and memory, we find the moment poignant but the freedom negligible. It makes no difference, we think, in that situation, his election of daring or of inhibition. Both are futile, without consequence. History sees no freedom for him, notes only constraint, labels him victim. But in the consciousness of that one man it makes great difference whether or not he experiences the choice. For if he knows the constraint and nothing else, if he thinks "Nothing is possible," then he is living his necessity; but if, perceiving the constraint, he turns from it to a choice between two possible courses of action, then—however he choose—he is living his freedom. This commitment to freedom may extend to the last breath.

IX

Ariana takes an apartment with a studio on Telegraph Hill, for days at a time does not go to San Anselmo. We spend evenings together, nights. Her painting changes, no more the dwarfs and giants and animals of her private world, but landscapes, children playing, many drawings of me. One day in her studio, hand full of brushes, she looks at a sketch of sailboats, sighs, drops her arms. "What do you think?" "I like it." "Well, I don't," she says, throws the brushes on a table. She stands by me, takes my arm, looks at it from a distance. "Strange, the things I do now . . . they are less interesting."

It's true. "Maybe you should bring back the dwarfs."

"I've tried," she says. "They won't come." She throws her arms around me. "But I don't care. I have you!"

We swim together, lie in the sun; in bed we read to each other, talk for hours. I rent a cabin in Big Sur and she brings prints, fabrics, paintings. On Friday afternoons we drive down the winding coast road, through the redwoods, over the high bridge; off the highway then on a rocky trail up the mountain till the car will go no further, then walk, carrying our supplies; have a view of the coast for fifty miles, day after day of clear skies, sunsets that fill the west with orange and red, nights of bright stars. She who had come to my bed in kindness is staying in love, and I who had taken her in loneliness and desire hold her now with a deepening feeling which I distrust.

Scott goes to Europe, Ariana doesn't know where he is. When we go to San Anselmo she is stricken at the rift in her life, moves about the house in a senseless agitation of worry, rearranging objects on the mantelpiece, wiping the dust with her fingers, rummaging through her desk, throwing away announcements, solicitations, then wondering what she is looking for, pausing, breaking her fingernails.

After work in the evening as I take off my coat in the hallway she comes in a swift movement of legs, a rhythm from the center flowing outward, a rustling of silk, warm arms around my neck, presses herself to me. "It's such a miracle," she says. "A finger, a hand, reaching up out of the current, pointing, touching me on the shoulder." She crouches, taps me with one finger. " 'You, there,' a voice says. 'You. Wake up! Wake, sleeper. It's not time to die.' And this hand, shaping itself out of the stream, takes my hand, pulls me back."

Her hand, as she catches mine, quivers; firelight plays on her face. In bed I drift toward sleep while she cherishes the moment, keeps it alive, caresses me, whispers, "I'm so happy. I really can't tell you." I feel her warmth around me, the dark hair in my face, the tangle of legs, the circle of arms.

On a clear cool night we lie on the ground outside the cabin at Big Sur. "How wonderful," she says. "Now, like this, no light but stars, no sound but crickets. Everything is transformed—trees, night, wind, smells . . . everything." The next day we pack a lunch, set out by foot toward the sea. A steep descent of several miles, no path. We clamber down cliffs, push through thickets, wade through a marsh, come finally upon a hidden beach, a stretch of gleaming sand cut off at either end by huge gray rocks which run out into the sea like the armored backs of dinosaurs. Just offshore is an island of rock against which the surf crashes.

No path gives upon this beach, no evidence of past visitors. We eat, lie on the warm sand, are lulled by the surf, sleep.

I have a dream about dying, wake with a start. Ariana is sitting beside me pouring sand through her fingers. She raises her eyes to mine. "I've been here before," she says, gestures vaguely at the beach. "Never thought to come back, didn't want to. Now . . . the wonderful land again. A second chance. Such a gift. I'm so grateful. I want to stay."

I too have been here before, the land of love, am dismayed to be here again. It's marvelous, lasts for a while, is necessary, everybody should come once—but I know the bitter end. She is bending over me, searching my face. "What are you thinking?" she says. Anxiety is in her eyes, I pull her to me so she can't see.

She walks away a few steps, begins to follow the receding waves, running back as they come up the beach, hair streaming in the wind. The tide is low now, the island connected to the shore by a spit of sand. Her motions become the ebb and flow of a wave, her arms and hair the pattern of foam. So small she is under the immense sky, so frail at the edge of the pounding ocean, ephemeral by the gray rocks. She comes back, reads my thoughts. "No, no," she says as I reach for her. Her dance changes now, teases. A scratch from the brush has left a line of blood on her calf. I chase her out on the spit where she dodges around the great boulders and when finally I catch her, breathless, we are both in water.

"Oh, look!" she cries as I pull her to me. Imbedded in the gray rock beside us is an iron spike holding a ring. Above it is a huge hook, nearby the initials "K.W.—A.I. 1889," almost obliterated. With her finger Ariana traces the faint letters. Thick flakes of rust fall to the sand as I lift the ring. She puts her hand through the ring with mine, escapes as I turn to kiss her. I stand there pondering the ring and hook, looking for clues; when a wave covers me with spray I start back. She is on a stretch of wet sand, runs as I come close, but further back on the beach lets me catch her, bear her down, presently finds my right hand with her left, locks our fingers, finds my eyes with hers, "Now! . . ."

I caress her temple with my lips, think of the initials in the rock. "It's too bad. I wanted us to be the first on this beach."

"I'm glad to share it," she says. "I like to think of her lying here, ruffled petticoats and pantaloons and high-laced shoes thrown in a pile on the sand. And I hope there were others—too taken up with making love to carve letters in stone—and others after us."

White clouds are mirrored in wet eyes.

One night in the cabin I wake from sound sleep, become aware of something dark, sweet, on my face, raise my hand; Ariana's hair. Her head lies in the crook of my arm, her breath warm on my chest. Something about the cabin is strange. I lift my head. Moonlight pours through the window, covers the bed with silver, throws a tracery of branches on a curve of thigh, on slight ankle and sleeping foot. She stirs, moans, snuggles against me.

I close my eyes to sleep but again feel strangeness. Has a noise waked me? I sit up, listen, hear only stillness. The image of pine needles on thigh is sharp, immobile. I go to the window. Nothing stirs, put on pants and coat, go outside. No chirp of cricket, no birdcall, no animal moves, no rustle of crawling thing. No plane in the sky, no bark of dog. Not a leaf turns. I walk under the trees, climb to the top of the hill, sit in dry grass. Below me the trees lie on the moonlit slope like hair on a sleeping face. A silver ribbon winds along the cliff above the sea. I see the roundness of the world, the ocean sloping off, falling. She may wake. I start back—stop. Something troubles me. A thought just missed, a memory veers from consciousness. I moved too soon; go back to the same spot, maybe still can find it.

What I want I have. What am I doing on a mountaintop? I move a few steps. Something takes my arm, pulls me back. If only I knew where to look . . . then come upon a stillness in myself. The night strikes me not with wonder, but recognition. It eludes me, flees any formulation. The clamor and dislocation are movement in the foreground, flight of time, while behind— unchanging landscape for the action of a play—unrelieved and unrelievable, lies stillness.

I shiver, feel a breeze on my face. The trees are stirring. Halfway down the hill, coming over a rise, I see light in the cabin, run the rest of the way, meet Ariana coming toward me. "What happened?" she cries, taking my shoulders.

"Nothing. I went for a walk."

"For a walk! Where? Why didn't you tell me?"

"You were sleeping. I didn't . . ."

"Oh, you! . . . I was frantic." She beats on me, begins to cry. "Don't ever do that again."

I hold her, stroke her hair. The wind is rising.

Between us is but one area of silence. When she thinks of Scott her voice changes, her expression grows anxious, she pulls at her eyebrows. She will get a divorce, but does not say when, won't talk about it. In May she gets a wistful card from Paris. "He's trying to make you feel guilty," I say, but can't console her. She starts to speak, shakes her head miserably, puts her hand on my arm in a sudden nervous gesture, breaks into tears. In June he returns but does not call. We hear from friends he is depressed. Twice Ariana goes to San Anselmo.

One evening he appears unannounced at the apartment on Telegraph Hill. Ariana is preparing dinner; she flushes, invites him to stay. He declines but sits, stretches out his legs, asks for a drink. It angers me to see how he affects her. He notices my mood, smiles in genial irony, shakes the ice in his glass.

"Why can't I work?" he says. "Why can't I do something? Such a wasteland." He speaks facetiously, rhetorically, watches us closely. "I lash out at myself. Invent! Invent! Make something interesting! Accept the meaninglessness of everything, that it makes no difference— still, invent, call out. Not in despair—what can anyone do but shrug, look away? But . . . so others will know they're not alone." His eyes probe at me. "I want to make wonderful comic films—about fear, loneliness, death—want to look in the eye of despair and laugh.

"But something stops me. Some obstacle . . . I feel it, don't know what it is."

We sit in silence. He finishes his drink. "What are you going to do?" Ariana asks.

"Why . . . press on," he says, grinning, "continue my search for something not permitted."

"There are plenty of limits," I say.

"Doubtless, but I can't find them. It seems to me I do what I want. I'm free, for example . . ." He looks about the apartment, eyes linger on Ariana, runs his hand lightly over her waist and hip. " . . . to take this away from you."

"Consider your search at an end," I say. "Ariana stays."

He comes directly before me, takes a small revolver from his inner coat pocket, cocks it, points it at me. Ariana screams. Scott looks at her, smiles, replaces the pistol. "Your no doesn't interest me," he says to me. "It's so easily put aside. I want to find a place where the universe says no, where I touch something hard." He grins mockingly. "And as for Ariana, I really might take her. I find myself wanting to fall unguardedly in love. I've been holding aloof for years, to protect my work. But that won't do. Without risk of hurt there's no love. Now I have nothing to protect, want back the passion, even the pain. So . . . watch out, Doctor!" He drains his glass again, raises his hand in salute. "Many thanks, chaps. It's been delightful. Come see me sometime," and he leaves.

Ariana is frantic. "Oh, Max! Do something for him!"

"I can't. He doesn't want to change."

"It's you who won't try," she says in sudden anger. "Why do you suppose he came here? You know something that could help him. He came to see *you*. You don't see any wish to change because you've got nothing to match it, and he won't show it for just nothing. You've given up on him. On everybody. I think you've given up on us."

I walk down Broadway, through the teeming Saturday night, the eager restless girls. How different my life now than when I prowled this street. What is this fighting about? I want her to hold me in the give and take of intimacy, yet be disinterested; divine my every need and meet it, as she largely does, but not notice how I chafe at the burden of her hope.

In my office the evening is still. Ariana's hand reaches here: a small silver dish with an inscription only I can understand, a copy of Klee's "Man on a Tightrope," an

Egyptian head in limestone no bigger than my thumb but five thousand years old, one cheek eroded, one ear missing, but the face serene. I listen, hear nothing, remember the stillness on the mountain, look down through the leather of shoes to feet, toenails twisted by fungus, through the wool of trousers to white hairy legs, knobby knees, wrinkled organs of shame and love and excrement—momentary configuration of energy in patternless clay. And what else? Some ties to patients, a few friends, Ariana. What more? A book, a few psychiatric papers, some scraps of research . . . a few faggots of meaning tied by a fraying cord, soon to be ashes.

X

In July, Ariana becomes absentminded, distracted by obscure promptings, looking or waiting for something. Scott goes away again. We stay in San Anselmo. The dwarfs come back, Ariana recovers in work.

One evening I find the house in darkness. "I'm here," she says from the living room as I let myself in. I sit beside her. She switches on the lamp, shows me a postcard. A Rodin sculpture, nude figures embracing, mailed in Paris: "Dear Wife. Home by October 15. Fair warning. Love and kisses. Scott."

"Why don't you stop running?"

"You seem so far away," she says. "I feel left out, terribly alone. There's a barrier. I keep pounding on it, trying to reach you . . . I can't."

On weekends we go to Big Sur, once for five days to Mexico. She is a museum of moods—passionate, indifferent, jolly, preoccupied. She does not speak of Scott; sometimes it seems he will never come back, that nothing will change. She gets another postcard, from Copenhagen this time, no mention of returning.

On the evening of October 17 we are on the green couch when the phone rings. She hesitates, turns to me nervously: "I'm afraid." After a moment she picks it up. "Hello. . . . No, no." A look of relief on her face. "Wrong number," she says, smiles helplessly, "I'm so pleased it wasn't Scott."

"It might have been. What are you going to do?"

"I don't know." She curls up against me. "Put your arms around me."

"What are you afraid of?"

"You. I'm not sure you love me. Really. . . . No, don't be impatient. Why do I have this doubt? You're everything I want, but you want more than me."

She brings her face close to mine. I pull out the hairpins, the black coil falls down her back. We turn off the lights, start up the stairs, arms around each other. There is a step on the porch, a key in the lock. Ariana becomes rigid. Scott is framed in the doorway. The hall light snaps on.

"Ah!" Scott says. "How sweet . . . and how surprised." We stand four steps up, staring down. "And how speechless! Aren't you glad to see me?"

After a moment Ariana goes down the steps, holds out her hand. "You might have let me know."

He pulls her to him, kisses her, watches me with mocking amusement over her lowered head. "There, my dear," he says. "That's enough. Your lover will take umbrage." He lets her go, and she steps away. "I think he already *has*. He doesn't say a word. What's this, old chap? No greeting for the cuckold?"

I go down the steps, hold out my hand. "Hello, Scott."

He stares at the hand, then my face. "But don't overdo it," he says with calm malice. "Hypocrisy is no doubt necessary, to lubricate the gears of society, but in moderation. No reason to shake the hand that plays with my wife's genitals."

He takes off his coat, goes to the living room. "It's good to be back. Charming room. Did I interrupt something? You are, I suppose, aware of my tact . . . no? I saw the light go out. I could have waited, discovered you *flagrante delicto*. Oh, I was tempted, I . . ."

"Let's go," I say to Ariana, taking her arm.

"Oh, do stay!" Scott says. "It would be lonely without

you." Ariana stares as if entranced; I put my arm around her. "That's sweet!" Scott says. "Charming."

Ariana takes my hand. "Come." Then to Scott, "I'll be back in a minute."

"Take your time. I do understand you two might have things to talk about."

In the car in darkness Ariana puts her arms around me. "Let me talk to him alone. Wait for me in San Anselmo."

I drive the three miles to town. Eleven o'clock and cold. I stop under a tree. The wind is blowing papers, there is a sprinkle of rain. After an hour I hear Ariana's car. She gets in beside me. "He's so sick," she says. "It breaks my heart."

"You can't be therapist to him," I say. "He wants to play cat and mouse. You're not safe there. I want you out."

"I will . . . as soon as I can. Give me a few days. I want to help him."

"You've got to give that up," I say angrily.

She weeps, I try to comfort her. Presently she opens the car door. "I have to go," she says.

She stays three days then comes to me in San Francisco.

In November, Scott is depressed, she visits him every day. In December, afraid for his life, she stays with him again. We see each other in snatched hours.

Christmas Eve is a gray day with banks of drifting fog, intermittent rain. I have no appointments, try to work at my desk. At ten Ariana telephones, her voice nervous and tired. I ask about Scott. "Oh . . . I don't want to talk about it. He just left. I'll see you . . . three o'clock. Usual place."

Again I try to work. Through the walls come festive sounds. Doors stand open, there is laughter and loud talk, much coming and going, occasionally a delighted squeal from a girl caught under mistletoe by the elevators. The bay is lead, the morning passes. There is a knock.

Scott enters. "Merry Christmas, Professor."

I gesture toward a chair, he shakes his head. "You are surprised," he says lightly, impersonally, as if remarking on a laboratory animal. "Well, I can't blame you." He closes the door slowly, rocks for a moment on heels and toes, glances at the bookshelves. His eyes come back to me, hands go to his pockets; I feel a touch of fear. "Well, Max . . . here we are. How are you?"

"All right."

"Ah . . . so. Wonderful." He moves desultorily along the wall, glancing at the books. I sit at my desk. "Sorry to find you alone, though. Particularly at Christmas. . . . Do I embarrass you? Surely we can be frank."

He watches me, to miss no twinge, I think. I raise a hand in annoyance. He turns away, withdraws a book, elaborately blows the dust, flips the pages. "You do seem rather touchy, Max. How *are* you anyway?"

"I'm well."

"Are you really? . . . I'm delighted, of course," he replaces the book, "but surprised. This must be a frustrating time. I've felt pretty bad kicking you out of my house. But . . . so it goes. I couldn't stay away forever just to make you comfortable."

I stand. "You'd better go."

His face is a mask, he turns, throws up his hands. "For months you avail yourself of the facilities of my house—bed and wife—here I am two minutes in your office . . . you throw me out. What's the matter? Conscience pricking you?"

I catch him by the shoulder, pull him around. "I won't stand for this."

"Ah!" he says softly. "How sensitive you are!"

He disengages my hand, continues the slow provocative tour of the room, picks up objects from my desk, tests the spring of the couch, tries out my analytic chair. At the window he stands hunched over, leaning against the frame, looking down—my own stance it occurs to me.

"Well," he says with a sigh, "let's drop it. If you want her . . . take her. She's pretty old, you know. Enjoy her in good health." He gives a short laugh. "Happy screwing."

He is at the door, eyes linger feverishly on mine, face hollow and haunted. Gibes are all he has left, and they're not enough; he's starving to death on a diet of sneers. "Try to take hold of yourself," I say. "It's not too late. Get yourself in treatment."

"There's something about me," he says "—damnedest thing—brings out the therapeutic in people . . . everybody." He raises a hand, leaves.

I call Ariana, no answer. My office is a cage, I can't work. A knock startles me. Must be her, I run for the door. A parcel. I stand there several minutes as if she might still appear.

Early in the afternoon I drive to San Anselmo, stop at the usual place. The town is empty—a few last-minute shoppers, the stores preparing to close. Water drips on the car. Three o'clock and she doesn't come. At three-thirty I drive to her house, pass slowly; the lights are on, both cars in the driveway. I go back to town, wait under the dripping tree, at four-thirty hear her car. She gets in beside me, hatless, taut face, open raincoat over black velvet dress, flings herself in my arms.

"Take me away," she says. "I can't go on this way. I'm so drained. It's too much." Her voice is high, about to break. I stroke the damp hair, she begins to relax.

"Scott came home drunk," she says, "lay on the bed,

wouldn't move, wouldn't talk. All he would say was, 'Get out.' Oh, Max!" She begins to cry.

I drive out of town on a dirt road, stop in a grove of eucalyptus. It is almost dark. On the seat between us she opens a box: sandwiches, fruitcake, almonds, a bottle of wine. Surprised to find myself hungry, I eat, am touched by her pleasure, when the wine is finished am sleepy. She opens her purse, gives me a gold watch, fastens it on my wrist. I take from my pocket a ring, wrought as a snake holding in its mouth a ball of jade. "I wish it were a wedding ring," I say, putting it on her finger.

Her face clouds. She pulls me to her, her face wet against mine, her hand at the back of my head, mouth seeking mine. I am averse but she persists, caressing, lips brushing my ear with a murmur. I begin to respond but am uneasy, the new watch ticking off the same hopeless progression. "Don't think about it," she whispers. "It will be all right. I want to give you something. Forget everything else." The soft lips move against my ear, the arms pull me to her. "Let me take you in. I love you." Qualms are falling away, she is over me, enveloping spirit in a loving whisper, body in ring of warmth.

I wake to find her asleep. My arm on which her head is lying is numb. She wakes with a start, recoils, screams. "Max! Max! . . . Is that you?" Finding me, realizing where she is, fear drains from her face, she moans, curls against me, puts her head on my chest. "Oh, darling. . . . Take me away."

But she won't come. She stays with Scott until late in January when, suddenly, he recovers. He begins a film, surrounds himself with people, and she comes back to me.

XI

Sometimes in therapy profound change occurs spontaneously, without effort or intention. It is a rare experience—any time, anywhere—to be known and understood without being judged, to be regarded with affection and respect, without being used. No therapist can feel this way about all his patients, though he must try. When he does genuinely so feel, he creates a nurturing context in which the patient may take in and make his own the therapist's way of thinking about problems, a certain reflectiveness about suffering, a tendency to hold conflicting motives in suspension while looking for connections, meanings, significance.

Such identification leads to slight, subtle, often unnoticed changes in action and behavior, in one's ways of dealing with one's self and others; and over a period of time these changed actions may achieve a change of being. One then feels one's self to be profoundly different without knowing how or why. If one is asked, "Well, what did you learn? What was the main insight?" one may stumble about, fabricate some inadequate answer, yet may know certainly that one is a better person, more able to love.

This sort of change is rare. We can't count on it, can't make it happen; when it occurs it is great good fortune, a bonus. Usually change—when it occurs at all—follows long and arduous trying.

Neurotic suffering indicates inner conflict. Each side of the conflict is likely to be a composite of many partial forces, each one of which has been structured into behavior, attitude, perception, value. Each component asserts itself, claims priority, insists that something else yield, accommodate. The conflict therefore is fixed, stubborn, enduring. It may be impugned and dismissed without effect, imprecations and remorse are of no avail, strenuous acts of will may be futile; it causes—yet survives and continues to cause—the most intense suffering, humiliation, rending of flesh. Such a conflict is not to be uprooted or excised. It is not an ailment, it is the patient himself. The suffering will not disappear without a change in the conflict, and a change in the conflict amounts to a change in what one is and how one lives, feels, reacts.

Personality is a complex balance of many conflicting claims, forces, tensions, compunctions, distractions, which yet manages somehow to be a functioning entity. However it may have come to be what it is, it resists becoming anything else. It tends to maintain itself, to convey itself onward into the future unaltered. It may be changed only with difficulty. It may be changed from within, spontaneously and unthinkingly, by an onslaught of physiological force, as in adolescence. It may be changed from without, again spontaneously and unthinkingly, by the force of unusual circumstance, as in a Nazi concentration camp. And sometimes it may be changed from within, deliberately, consciously, and by design. Never easily, never for sure, but slowly, uncertainly, and only with effort, insight, and a kind of tenacious creative cunning.

Personality change follows change in behavior. Since we are what we do, if we want to change what we are we must begin by changing what we do, must undertake a new mode of action. Since the import of such action is change it will run afoul of existing entrenched forces which will protest and resist. The new mode will be experienced as difficult, unpleasant, forced, unnatural, anxiety-provoking. It may be undertaken lightly but can be sustained only by a considerable effort of will. Change will occur only if such action is maintained over a long period of time.

The place of insight is to illumine: to ascertain where one is, how one got there, how now to proceed, and to what end. It is a blueprint, as in building a house, and may be essential, but no one achieves a house by blueprints alone, no matter how accurate or detailed. A time comes when one must take up hammer and nails. In building a house the making of blueprints may be delegated to an architect, the construction to a carpenter. In building the house of one's life or in its remodeling, one may delegate nothing; for the task can be done, if at all, only in the workshop of one's own mind and heart, in the most intimate rooms of thinking and feeling where none but one's self has freedom of movement or competence or authority. The responsibility lies with him who suffers, originates with him, remains with him to the end. It will be no less his if he enlists the aid of a therapist; we are no more the product of our therapists than of our genes: we create ourselves. The sequence is suffering, insight, will, action, change. The one who suffers, who wants to change, must bear responsibility all the way. "Must" because so soon as responsibility is ascribed, the forces resisting change occupy the whole of one's being, and the process of change comes to a halt. A psychiatrist may help, perhaps crucially, but his best help will be of no avail if he is required to provide a kind or degree of insight which will of itself achieve change.

Should an honest man wish to become a thief the necessary action is obvious: he must steal—not just once or occasionally, but frequently, consistently, taking pains that the business of planning and executing thefts replaces other activities which in implication might oppose the predatory life. If he keeps at it long enough his being will conform to his behavior: he will have become a thief. Conversely, should a thief undertake to become an honest man, he must stop stealing and must undertake actions which replace stealing, not only in time and energy, and perhaps also excitement, but which carry implications contrary to the predatory life, that is, productive or contributive activities. If a homosexual should set out to become heterosexual, among all that is obscure, two things are clear: he should discontinue homosexual relations, however much tempted he may be to continue on an occasional spontaneous basis, and he should undertake, continue, and maintain heterosexual relations, however little heart he may have for girls, however often he fail, and however inadequate and averse he may find himself to be. He would be well advised in reaching for such a goal to anticipate that success, if it be achieved at all, will require a long time, years not months, that the effort will be painful and humiliating, that he will discover profound currents of feeling which oppose the behavior he now requires of himself, that emerging obstacles will each one seem insuperable yet each must be thought through, that further insight will be constantly required to inform and sustain his behavior, that sometimes insight will precede and illumine action, and sometimes blind, dogged action must come first, and that even so, with the best of will and good faith and determination, he still may fail. He should beware of beckoning shortcuts, such as drug therapy or hypnosis. They falsify the reality with which he must most intimately deal, that of his own thought, feeling, drive;

they undermine his commitment of internal resources by encouraging him to feel that there is an easier way. There is no shortcut, no safe conduct, no easier way. He must proceed alone, on nerve. He is not entitled to much hope— just that he has a chance. He may take some bleak comfort only in knowing that no one can be sure at the outset that he will fail, and that it is his own unmeasured and unmeasurable resources of heart and mind and will which have most bearing on the eventual outcome.

This is self-transcendence and is not to be confused with a type of coercive treatment in which the therapist acts as agent for society, and the goal is adjustment. Punishment, brainwashing, and lobotomy fall in this category. Less extreme varieties are known variously as operant conditioning, behavior therapy, or conditioned reflex therapy. All such treatment takes the person as object and seeks to achieve the desired change by manipulation. The alcoholic may be so rigged with wires as to receive an electric shock each time he takes a drink. The homosexual man may be provided with male partners who insure that sexual experiences will be exceedingly unpleasant, and, concurrently, with gently seductive ladies, without demands of their own, who introduce him to the delights of polarized sexuality. Such things may be arranged for a fee.

We are in no position to comment on the efficacy of behavior therapy as generally practiced, but in principle we know it works. People may indeed be treated as objects and may be profoundly affected thereby. Kick a dog often enough and he will become cowardly or vicious. Men who are kicked undergo similar changes; their view of the world and of themselves is transformed. The survivors of Hitler's concentration camps testify that the treatment received did have an effect. Nor find we any reason to doubt the alleged results of Chinese thought-control methods. People may indeed be brainwashed, for benign or exploitative reasons.

Behavior therapy is not, therefore, being contrasted with self-transcendence in terms of efficacy; the contrast is in terms of freedom. If one's destiny is shaped by manipulation one has become more of an object, less of a subject, has lost freedom. It matters little whether the manipulation is known to the person upon whom it acts. For even if one himself designs and provides for those experiences which are then to affect him, he is nevertheless treating himself as object—and to some extent, therefore, *becomes* an object.

If, however, one's destiny is shaped from within then one has become more of a creator, has gained freedom. This is self-transcendence, a process of change that originates in one's heart and expands outward, always within the purview and direction of a knowing consciousness, begins with a vision of freedom, with an "I want to become . . .," with a sense of the potentiality to become what one is not. One gropes toward this vision in the dark, with no guide, no map, and no guarantee. Here one acts as subject, author, creator.

Sometimes a process of character change may proceed with increasing momentum and finality to solid completion. The honest man becomes the complete thief; the thief becomes the completely honest man. When character change proceeds to such radical conclusion it is likely, not only that the old way of life has been given up, but also that a new way of life, directly opposite in implication, has been adopted. Such a change is experienced, not as a deflection of course, but as an absolute turning around, a conversion, may even call for a change of name. Saul of Tarsus had such an experience on the road to Damascus and—having been the chief persecutor of Christianity—became its greatest exponent. Malcolm X had such an experience in prison with the teachings of Elijah Muhammad, and changed not simply from thief to nonthief, but from thief to social reformer; the completeness and finality with which he transcended the old identity owed as much to his having undertaken with passion and commitment to correct injustice as it did to his giving up of stealing. Had he simply "learned his lesson," decided not to steal any more, and taken an indifferently regarded job as gas station attendant he may never have altogether ceased being a thief. Some of the temptation, bitterness, and envy, something of the way of thought, attitude, and outlook of a thief may have remained.

Such change as occurred in Saul or Malcolm X is rare, seems so far beyond anything we might expect to achieve by our own efforts that, when it occurs, we usually ascribe credit—to a mystic force, to a revelation, to the hand of God. Such changes as we achieve with ourselves, with or without therapy, are likely to be partial and provisional. The homosexual gets married, has children, but never feels entirely safe with women; the frigid woman becomes capable of climax, but not easily and not always; the impotent man becomes able usually to make it, but can never be sure; the depressive character can work, may occasionally feel glad to be alive, but is not likely ever to be described as of sunny disposition; the phobic woman becomes less anxious, no longer has to decline invitations, but always has sweaty palms at cocktail parties. Such changes must be counted success; for more frequent in outcome, even with considerable effort, is no change at all.

He who undertakes to transform himself, therefore, should think not of all or none, sick or well, miserable or happy, but of more or less, better or worse. He should undertake only to do what he can, to handle something better, to suffer less. The kingdom of heaven need not concern him.

When the thief takes a job and determines to go straight, when the homosexual gets a girl and renounces sexual relations with men, he does so with a vision of what he will become. Rarely may such direct action, in the course of time and of great effort, succeed without further insight and with no change of plan. More often the course upon which one has embarked entails so much anxiety, uncertainty, confusion, that reappraisal becomes necessary. One finds that his entire self was not known, that submerged aspects of self now rise up in terror, threat, and subversion, screaming outrage, demanding revocation. One is forced to halt, sometimes driven back. The whole issue has to be rethought. "What I'm giving up is more important than I knew." "Maybe I don't want to change." "Am I going at it the wrong way?" Newly emerging feelings and reactions must be explored in relation to other known elements and to one's now threatened intention.

Here therapy may offer insight into bewildering experience, help with the making of new connections, give comfort and encouragement, assist in the always slippery decision of whether to hang on and try harder or to look for a different way to try. That person gains most from therapy, and gains it most quickly, who has the heart and will to go it alone in the event that therapy does not help; whereas he who clings to therapy as drowning man to ship's timber is more likely to burden therapy with a weight it can't support, and so take himself and therapy down together.

XII

We are in bed at Ariana's apartment when the phone
rings. Scott has been arrested, is in jail. We dress, drive to
the Hall of Justice. At the desk I ask the charge. "Battery,"
the sergeant says, and indicates a woman sitting on a bench
in the far corner. It's Zoë. She wears a prison wrapper, has
a swollen eye turning blue, blood on her lips. Her body
tenses as I approach. She glares, pants, raises her hands like
claws, as if to spring. "What happened?" I ask.

She leaps up, shakes her fists. "Pig! Pig! Pig!" points to
her eye. The sergeant laughs. Zoë turns on him, shrieks,
waves her arms. "He was chasing her down Columbus
Avenue," the sergeant says.

Zoë beats on my chest for attention, throws open her
wrapper, displays a bruise on her thigh. With shrill
protestation she points to other injuries of which I see no
evidence, all the while gesticulating wildly. A large man
enters. He wears a black suit, black shirt without tie, black
hat, has a dark, impassive face, an unlighted cigar in his
mouth. The bouncer at the Port Said, Ariana says. Zoë runs
to him, yelling over her shoulder, cursing, not me
apparently but Scott. She tears off the prison wrapper,
throws it on the floor with a contemptuous toss of her
head, spits, slips into the fur coat which the bouncer holds
for her, glowers at Ariana. They leave.

I arrange bail and we are allowed to see Scott, find him
behind bars, barefooted, naked above the waist. His

expression, poised between levity and panic, undergoes visible relief as he sees us.

"Has the universe said no to you yet?" I ask. He grins ruefully, shakes his head. I rap the steel bars. "Isn't this hard enough?"

At that moment the warden unlocks the door, and Scott walks out with impish triumph, turns up his palms, shrugs mockingly. "She's out of her mind," he says to Ariana. "We were playing." His cocky manner does not entirely conceal his quaking. Ariana is wordless, pale, looks at him with helpless, anguished stare. Scott turns to me. "We were playing," he says again.

"On Columbus Avenue?"

He grins. "That wasn't very wise, was it? We ran smack into a police car."

"And the black eye?"

"Rough games," he says.

I give him my raincoat. Ariana still has said nothing. In the car she moves toward me, making room for him on the front seat. "Where do you want to go?" I ask.

"To Zoë's."

"You won't be very welcome."

"Come . . . with us," Ariana says. Her voice is unfamiliar, metallic.

"Oh, good," Scott says. "Shall we have an orgy?"

"You are not coming with us," I say angrily. "Where do you want to go?"

"I told you," he says mildly, "to Zoë's."

"Go home, Scott," I say. "I'll take you. Zoë is very angry."

"She's volatile," he says, "it doesn't last."

I drive to Columbus Avenue. He points out her

apartment, two lighted windows on the fourth floor of a building near Broadway. "She's there now," he says. "I see her shadow on the ceiling."

"Please don't," Ariana says.

"A lovers' quarrel," he says. "Don't worry."

"I'm afraid," she says. "Please . . . come with us."

He walks away with a wave, enters the building. I start to drive off. "No," Ariana says, taking my arm. "Go in with him, please!"

"Leave him alone. You can't . . ."

She fumbles with the door handle. "Stop. Let me out."

I leave the car in a red zone. "Stay here," I say to her, and follow Scott into the house. The hall is dimly lighted by a single bulb. On an iron cot near the stairwell a man with a black beard is snoring. I walk up two flights, am starting on the third when I hear Scott's voice, presently see him standing before a closed door. Zoë's continuing tirade, muted by the door, rises and falls as she walks about her room. Furniture is being moved, she's putting things back in order. I stop unnoticed on the stairs. Whenever there is a lull in the ranting Scott indicates his penitent presence, tries the knob.

"Let me in, baby . . . please . . . I won't hurt you, won't touch you . . . I'll rub it . . . make it all right . . . will do anything. . . ."

Zoë's curses subside into scolding, the pauses become longer, her heels on the floor less furious. When Scott tries the door again it opens on the chain. For a moment she appears at the crack, shouts at him.

"We'll go shopping tomorrow," Scott says.
"Gumps . . . Saks . . . a new
dress . . . bracelets . . . those Bally shoes. . . ."

She appears once more, putting dresses on hangers. The chain is lifted, Scott enters. The door is closed and locked.

I go downstairs. The bearded man is still sleeping. No mattress, he lies on the springs, mouth open, smelling of warm urine. As I open the front door I see Ariana across the street, white, suffering. A drunk staggers at the curb, taps on the car window, tries to engage her in conversation. She pays no attention, is watching for me. As I cross the sidewalk a window opens, I look up, see two heads leaning out. "Hey, lover boy!" Scott holds out my coat, drops it. It floats down, is caught for a moment on electric wires, is freed by the wind, falls to the sidewalk. "Thanks for the drapes," he calls. "Drive carefully. Don't stay out late. Be gentle with my wife." They laugh and wave. Scott blows a kiss to Ariana. Passers-by smile as I pick up my coat.

We sit on the couch in my room. The sun is a pulsating orange about to touch the water, above it horizontal bands of gold, red, pale green. An enormous pink sky. A carrier slides silently under the web of black threads and out to sea. From the phonograph the *Heiliger Dankgesang* of the A minor quartet. Slowly the water darkens to ink.

When the phone rings Ariana jerks forward. "No!" It breaks my heart, this hidden terror. I rub her neck. She sighs, puts her face in her hands. "It's just the phone," I say. "Too much," she says, her voice small, muffled by hands.

I pick up the phone, look down on her curved back, see the muscles stiffen to Scott's voice. "Hello, chaps!" he says. "Out of bed now! Too early for that. Come to a 'happening' in Berkeley. Public performance. Zoë is going to dance in the raw. Great show, you can't miss it." Ariana shakes her head, I tell him no. He insists, gives me the address, says he'll send a car. I hang up.

"I wish we could go away," she says slowly, then turns to me in desperation. "Don't let me go."

In bed she leans over me, tensed for some hidden onslaught. Her hair moves over my face. "Why so frantic, sweetheart?"

"Because . . . it can all be lost . . . everything."

I am stroking her breast when she sees something in my face. "What's the matter?" she says anxiously. "What are you thinking?" I pull her down. I had begun to think, as so often, of those tangled roots, wonder what Scott has done to her, how he has posed her, doing what . . . with whom.

She moves suddenly. "Can we go away? Would you? Right now." She sits up, is upset that I don't believe her to be serious.

"Impossible. How would we live? My patients . . . I can't just disappear."

"Call them," she says, "right now. Call each one. Say . . . an emergency, you have to leave immediately, can't return, refer them to someone else."

"There's no emergency. I can't lie to them."

"How do you know?" she says. "Real emergencies may be like this. Nothing . . . the sun going down, an ordinary day, the sky getting dark, everything as usual. But something bad coming on, sensed . . . but if you know it, it *is* an emergency, not a lie."

I laugh. "There's no emergency, I have no intuition, it's simply impossible to go like that."

She sighs, gives up. I pet her, she won't turn to me. "It

would take time," I say. "We would have to plan what to do, where to go. Many things to consider."

We lie in bed, the sky is dark, the stars are out. She becomes cold, pulls up a blanket. I too am cold, also bored, annoyed with her impulsive demand which spoiled our mood. I get up, walk about. After a while she starts to prepare dinner, is listless, desultory. We discover that neither of us is hungry.

"Shall we go to Scott's 'happening'?" I say.

"All right," she says distantly. I am astonished that she agrees, and am suddenly dismayed at myself for having suggested it.

At the hall in Berkeley, Scott meets us at the door, reaches out as if to pat Ariana on the cheek, but is unsteady, misses her face, catches her ear instead. He has something in his hand, perhaps a fingernail clipper, cuts her ear slightly. She cries out, I knock his hand away, there is left a trace of blood. He mumbles something, his eyes are glazed, he wanders away. It is not clear exactly what happened, whether he meant it or not.

Weird music fills the hall, shrill, screaming, unearthly. We find seats, are surrounded by young women with loose flowing hair, by men young and old with beards. Several have taken off their shirts. The light is dim, the air heavy with smoke, incense, marijuana, sweat. Three walls are hung with sheeting, the fourth with a gauze curtain. Ariana clings to my arm, trembles; I find nothing, no one, that mirrors us; we should not be here.

The lights fade, the movies begin. On one wall copulating animals—dogs, cats, dolphins, elephants—the sound track carrying snarls, roars, and screams. Presently the sound fades though the pictures continue, and now on

the opposite wall begins a war film: tanks burning, cities
being bombed, mines exploding, ships sinking, soldiers
bayoneting soldiers. The spectacle of war continues as the
sound fades, and now on the back wall begins a film of
leaders addressing multitudes of cheering followers:
Mussolini, Hitler, Roosevelt, Pius XII, Stalin, Churchill. On
the ceiling begins a film of human lovemaking—a tangle of
arms and legs, mouths that writhe, suck, and struggle on
each other, blind, fishlike—with the sighs, grunts, and
groans of orgasm. All heads are on end, beards point up
like erect members, faces yearn toward the illusory ceiling.
Now all sound tracks play together, faces turn this way
and that: a male tiger lunges into a snarling female jaguar,
S.S. men machine-gun Polish Jews, Hitler screams from the
Brandenburg Gate, while on the ceiling a fat salivating
woman raps out a staccato ecstasy. To these sounds now is
added electronic music. The volume increases. People
begin to sway and groan, some roll on the floor. Ariana, in
pain, sits with lowered head, hands over her ears. Behind
the gauze curtain the stage is lighted, Zoë dances naked
before a huge papier-mâché phallus.

A red light flashes: house lights come up, Zoë vanishes,
the movies end. Only the music continues. People stand
up, mill about. Policemen enter. The music tapers weirdly
up to a single, shrill, head-splitting note, remains fixed. I
take Ariana away.

Scott sees us leave, catches us outside on the sidewalk.
"Come with me," he says thickly, taking our arms.
"Friend's house, private showing . . . very special movies."

"No," I say, and push away his hand.

"Please come home," Ariana says.

"Couldn't possibly. Evening's just started." He shakes his
head, backs away. "So long, chaps. We'll miss you. Have a
romp!" He waves, re-enters the hall.

We drive in silence to Ariana's apartment. Nothing is right. In bed we can't make love, are restless, toss about, sigh, grumble. "What are you mad about?" she says finally.

"You've got to stop hanging on to him. Leave him alone."

"Don't torment me!" she cries out, slamming her hand on the bed. "You want me totally . . . the past too, but moment to moment. You don't believe in us . . . in anything, want me to give up every tie, every person—but for what? Not for love. You don't believe in love."

She cries. I leave in anger.

On Columbus Avenue near Broadway I am stopped by a pack of cars, people in the street looking up. I follow their gaze, see Zoë's lighted room, white ceiling. The window is open; a gauze curtain streams out and up, undulates, a licking tongue. Then, to the left of the window, I see a woman on a ledge. It is Zoë, naked, precariously lodged. She presses herself flat, hair blows in the wind, hands grope the wall behind her. She stares at the growing crowd, shrinks back, raises a hand as if in hatred and suspicion. A police car with wailing siren gets through by driving on the sidewalk. An officer enters the building, another holds back the crowd. More sirens, policemen forcing cars to move on. I manage to get my car to the curb, leap out, wave both arms, yell, "Zoë! Go back!" More sirens, police whistles, automobile horns, a fire truck coming up slow in the cluttered street. Zoë edges further to the left. I continue to shout. "Go back! The other way! Zoë! Go back!" She doesn't hear me, recoils from the crowd below. People stare from every window, from all the buildings, both sides of the street. A net is being readied. Before it arrives she raises her arms, screams something, shakes her fists, loses her footing. The crowd gasps. Someone beside me claws at my shoulder, sighs deeply. She struggles as she falls, extends her arms as if imploring God, throws back her head in vehement plea, arches spine, impacts on concrete.

I break through. She lies spread-eagled on her back. I kneel beside her, the head is crushed. Before the blanket covers her I see whip marks on her belly. Her heart is beating, but she doesn't breathe. The ambulance has arrived and I go with her, my mouth on hers, her breast rising to my breath while the siren wails and city lights flicker and spin beyond the window, my left hand under her neck, covered with blood, holding her head extended, my right hand under her breast, feeling the beat of heart become weaker and weaker, thready, begin to miss, stop. I massage the heart under the rib cage: it beats once . . . then again . . . then no more. She is dead on arrival at the Mission Emergency.

It is three o'clock when I get back to Ariana's apartment, let myself in. She is not here, the impression of her head lies in the pillow. The covers have been thrown back, a glass of water overturned by the phone, her nightgown is on the floor. I telephone Scott's house, then my own apartment; no answer either place.

I drive to San Anselmo. No light as I come out of the redwoods, no moon, a black night, but as I turn in the driveway Scott's Lancia is in my headlights. The doorbell rings loud, as in a house without curtains or rugs. No one comes but I know he's there, know he's awake. I ring long, like an alarm, then short. Finally footsteps and Ariana, with a small flashlight, opens the door.

"So you know," I say.

"You should not be here."

"Let me in."

"No. Go away please. The police may come. I'll call you tomorrow." She tries to close the door.

"Wait!" I block the door with my foot, angry. "Why are you here?"

"In case he's questioned . . . I came with him directly here, from Berkeley."

"So you'd perjure yourself."

"Oh, my dear," she moans, "don't make it harder."

She covers her face with her hands, sways toward me. Behind her, at the top of the stairs, a light is turned on. Scott, with frightened face, peers down. "Ariana!" he whispers. "Ariana!" Through her straight-hanging gown I see the curve of hip, breast.

"Why are you undressed?" I say. She moans, leans against the door. Scott, frightened by the sound, snaps off the light. "Do you have to be in bed with him to establish his alibi?"

She takes her hands from her face, looks at me, appalled. "Leave me alone. Leave me alone."

The sky is red over Mount Diablo as I come down the Waldo Grade, mine is the only car on the ghostly bridge. I think of last evening, the sky red then in the west, the bands of color, of Ariana's thigh as we watched the pulsing sun—how much to happen in one night!—of Zoë's shapeless mouth under mine, Ariana stopping me at the door like a stranger—like a salesman!—feel murder for Scott, for all he has taken away.

In my apartment I lie down but can't sleep. It's daylight. I get up, straighten my office, drink coffee, try to eat. At eight-thirty I begin to see patients, feel close to them today, find in myself the same need for someone to turn to that they have for me. The quality of misery is different in each, but each hurts, and I too. I want to help, and do, and this helps me, and I feel fortunate to be so trusted, yet vaguely guilty, uneasy, can't forget Ariana closing the door, dread I'm losing her.

At ten-thirty, between patients, a newscast reports the suicide. My eleven-thirty patient, a member of the Sexual Freedom League of Berkeley, talks about a gangbang on Zoë after the "happening," ascribes it to Scott. I feel responsible for him, for Zoë's death.

At lunch I have a free hour, call San Anselmo, wait a long time as the phone rings. I imagine them looking at each other, anxious, unmoving. I go then to Ariana's apartment, find it exactly as it was at three o'clock. I pick up her nightgown, walk about the rooms holding it to my face. The breakfast table is set for two, egg cups on white doilies, coffee cups inverted—a sitting down together that time passed over. I had left in anger, she had left in fear, no one here now but ghosts. Not even I am here. Everything is changed. I'm a visitor as at Pompeii, looking in on a life that was lived long ago, but from which strangely the actors have just fled. A moment earlier and I would have heard the dying footfalls, mine and hers, the trailing voices. Yet it's an ancient silence fills the rooms.

I am startled by a key in the lock, step back, thinking the police have come. It is Ariana—gray silk suit, slim waist, moving slowly in the flickering greenish light and the slowed time of a dream, and I think how beautiful she is, how marvelously she walks. She is closing the door as she sees me, cries out, shrinks back, hand to mouth.

In my arms she feels crumpled, smaller, her head folded down on my chest. I hold her a long time, cannot make her respond, have again the terrible sense that everything has changed.

"I've come to pack a bag," she says finally, freeing herself. "He's in a panic, says he's falling."

"So? . . . Why must *you* nurse him? Why so tender?" She lowers her face. "And speaking of 'falling'—what about Zoë? Does she count for nothing?"

Ariana shakes her head. "I can't leave him now." She goes in the bedroom, I follow. She takes clothes from the closet.

"We have to commit him," I tell her.

"No," she says, as if she had considered it. "Would do no good."

"Would keep him from killing someone else."

"He didn't kill her."

"Aren't you being technical?"

"She was seen to jump. He wasn't in her room."

"Beside the point," I say. "You know he's sick, is dangerous, you know he's got to be confined."

"I would if it would help, but not to get rid of him."

I take her shoulders, shake her. "Ariana, we *have* to."

"Leave me alone!"

I watch gloomily as she finishes packing. Her face is dark, unhappy, as she closes the case and comes to stand beside me. "When will I see you?" I say.

"I'll call you."

She kisses me on the cheek, leaves. For a while longer I stay there in the past, with the ghosts, in the apartment in Pompeii. In the distance someone is practicing the guitar.

XIII

A day passes, another. She doesn't call. On the third day
I determine not to call her, go that night to North Beach
to find a girl, thinking I'll take her to Ariana's apartment
and bed. What I find in a din of jazz is a nineteen-year-old
Haitian with short curly hair, red lips, round expressionless
face. I change my mind about where to take her, give the
driver my own address. In the cab I don't touch her,
neither of us speaks. I think of the brown couch in my
apartment, the gray chair in the bedroom where Ariana
leaves her clothes, see her white slip with lace, the
stockings, the bra sliding to the floor, her presence on
everything. I glance at the girl. "What's your name?"
"Jeanine." She wears a red jersey dress, very tight, reaches
only to midthigh; I see it thrown across the gray chair—
lean forward suddenly, "Driver, take us to the West Wind
Motel."

I lock the door, sit on the bed, think of the tricks she
may know, but can't respond, watch sadly as she peels the
tight dress up over her head. Black satin skin with scarlet
traverses: red bikini with black lace, tiny red bra which
just covers nipples and areolae. The lithe body lazily
bumps and grinds. She raises her arms, turns around,
hunches shoulders forward, the bra falls, she pushes down
the bikini; but it's not for me, I pull her to the bed, try to
make conversation. She's restive, wants to work on me. I
shake my head, tell her to get dressed. Her feelings are
hurt, and paying doesn't help; she leaves without a word

and I find myself sitting on the bed in pants and undershirt, staring senselessly at a glass in a wax paper bag, feeling things are going awry, something important is slipping, don't know how to stop it, and whatever I try becomes a flailing about that makes it worse.

The next afternoon I cancel my patients, drive to San Anselmo. The day is warm, sunny, windless. The yard before the Craig house is a sea of daffodils, flame tulips along the walk. Ariana has heard the car, comes from around the house to meet me, wears a sleeveless dress with broad diagonal stripes of black and white, takes my arm, for a moment puts her head on my shoulder. Strain has lined her face, she has not slept, I think. Minute drops of perspiration stand in the down of her lip. We do not speak, she holds my arm tightly. I feel sorry for her as we walk around the house to the patio.

A small table is set with yellow brocade cloth, a vase of daffodils, tea service—a scene from Chekhov. "Country life has its charms," I say. "Very cozy."

Ariana flushes, brings another chair. Scott stands awkwardly, holds out his hand. Wants to be forgiven, wants everything the same. "Have the police come yet?" I ask, dismissing the hand with a shake of my head.

"Yes."

"And what did you tell them?"

"Nothing."

"Did they ask about those marks on Zoë's belly?"

"I knew nothing."

"So you lied."

"You think I owe honesty to policemen?"

Ariana has brought another cup and plate, another napkin of yellow brocade. I sit on a yellow vinyl cushion which sighs under my weight, a chair of white wrought-iron tracery like lace. Tea is poured, a plate of *petits fours* is passed. I can't reconcile this scene with Zoë's body, the crushed head, the matted hair. One or the other is unreal, is a lie—and it's this one. I drink the tea, eat the pastry, become furious, as if tricked into taking the sacrament of a religion I despise. Ariana makes efforts at conversation which Scott picks up hysterically; I am silent. After a while Ariana gives up, sits across from me with lowered head. Scott is intensely nervous, puts his hand on hers, his soft white fingers making quick entreaties. Her brown hand does not respond but is not withdrawn, and this weight of him on her, and her acceptance of it, goads me.

"I have things to tell you, Scott. Alone." I have to get away from this absurd, insulting table. "Come for a walk with me."

"I . . . well. . . ." Again he puts his soft wet hand on hers. "Will you come?" he whispers.

She looks at him calmly. "He wants to talk to you alone."

Scott stands with a sudden jerk, still holding her hand. I stand. "No! No!" he says shrilly. "I won't go." He sits again, just as suddenly. "You can say it here. Whatever it is. I have no secrets from my wife."

"No, just from the police, you bastard! And have the insufferable nerve to say 'my wife,' to brag of a frankness you've never used except to torment her—except now when you use it in fear." In lieu of hitting him I jerk my chair from the table, overturning it.

A bee buzzes around the daffodils. Ariana pays no attention, Scott flails at it.

"All right," I say, "we'll talk here. You are sick, you have to go to a hospital."

"Ariana and I have discussed that," he says—I recognize a prepared speech. "I've given it a lot of thought . . . have decided not to go."

"He did consider it," Ariana says, "kept it open till today."

"When did the police come?" I ask.

"Yesterday," Ariana says.

"But of course! If they'd had something on him he'd go—as a dodge. If he's in the clear, he won't."

"I won't go," Scott says in an effort at dignity, "because I'm not sick."

"You are not competent to judge," I snap.

"Are you," he says, "as my wife's lover, competent?"

He has scored, better watch my temper. "You are sick in a way that makes you dangerous, that was fatal for Zoë."

"That's a charge, not a diagnosis."

"I'm not going to argue with you, Scott. It's not necessary. You *know* you're sick. The only question is what to do about it. You want to play around. I'm *telling* you: you have to go to a hospital."

"No."

I look at Ariana: head lowered, miserable, abstaining. "If you won't go willingly, you have to be committed."

"You can't do that. Only a court . . ."

"Yes, only a court. But a court *will*."

"I don't think so." His voice is rising. "I'll have the best lawyer, I'll . . ."

"You will be in more trouble," I say, "if you are judged sane. Then there will be criminal charges."

"They've got nothing on me," he shrills. "She was not forced. Everything was for pleasure."

I feel sick. "You push the limits of pleasure rather far, don't you?"

His chin is trembling. Ariana looks at her folded hands as in a trance. The bee buzzes before us in the daffodils. After a while I walk around the house to the car, sit behind the wheel. Ariana comes, stands beside me.

Inside the house Scott looks out at us, moves from window to window. I take Ariana's hand, draw her into the car. "Come with me," I plead. "I can't leave you here."

Scott comes flying out. "Go back," she says to him, as to a child; "I'm not leaving." He hesitates. "Go in the house," she says firmly; "I'll be there soon."

Reluctantly, with backward glances, he obeys. Again moves from room to room, watching.

"You can't help him," I say.

"I have to try."

"You've tried for ten years and he's become more and more the sadist. You can't give him anything new. He wants only to hide behind your skirts till he's over this scare."

"Will a hospital help him?"

"I don't know, I . . ."

"What do you think?" she insists. "Really? . . ."

I hesitate. "I think nothing will help him."

I try to draw her to me, but she sits straight. Inside the house Scott moves from window to window. I look at her face, the clear profile, the curve of lashes, the line of nose; run my hand through the soft black hair, see it below me on white sheet. "I can't let you stay. It's not safe." She looks straight ahead. A jet passes over us, northbound for Seattle. "I'd have some hope if he felt guilt, but he doesn't, just fear." Still no reply.

"I have to go now," she says after a while.

I take her arm. "If you won't commit him, I'll have to do it without you."

"Please don't!"

"I have to. I can't just forget what happened . . . what could happen to you."

She searches my face, kisses me, walks slowly back to the house.

I do nothing about Scott that day, or the next, and the longer I wait the more difficult it becomes. With the signature of one other psychiatrist I can have him picked up. Whom shall I ask? Lars? Julian? Can I, without disclosing my involvement, ask anyone? Perhaps I must disqualify myself altogether, ask the two of them to do it. But would they not turn me down, discounting the danger to Ariana as the apprehensiveness of a lover, or, if I insist, refer me to the police? I could sign a complaint as friend of the family . . . but with the wife opposed, that would come to nothing.

But suppose, somehow, I *do* get him picked up. He could be held for three days against his will in the County Hospital. What then? The judge would have to rule. And might not commit. I imagine Scott explaining himself to the judge—the cultivated speech, the achievements in film, his great distress at Zoë's suicide, the disclosure of my affair with his wife—"Case dismissed!" At that point, indeed, the judge might ask the State Medical Board to look into my professional deportment. The more carefully I consider what to do the more empty my threats seem to have been; I'm dismayed to find that my involvement has robbed me of authority. Yet I know for sure he is dangerous.

I consider going to the police. But with what evidence?
I can't prove it was he who used the whip. And if I could
it wouldn't hold him long. The orgy is hearsay. I could
destroy the alibi Ariana has provided, but could not
establish that he was in Zoë's room, nor ever know what
happened there before she climbed out on the ledge. I
could have him questioned again, perhaps locked up for a
few hours, and that's all. His menace is as much too subtle
for the law as for psychiatry.

When I have finished with my patients on the third day
I begin packing a suitcase before I realize fully the
decision I have come to: If Ariana won't leave, if I can't
tear Scott away, then I must join them. It amuses me that
Ariana will see nothing odd in this, will find it natural that
I should move in to help her. I will be the doctor, she the
nurse—a mental hospital for one. Rather exclusive care
Scott will have arranged for himself, but in his style; he
never travels second-class. As I cross the bridge I think
how incredulous my colleagues would be, how
disapproving the State Medical Board: to treat the husband
of my mistress in his own home. Yet the more I think of it
the more possible it seems, perhaps because I can imagine
no other course. I even feel hopeful—not for fundamental
change, but to get him on his feet. And who knows?
Maybe a little more. At least to the point of not clinging to
Ariana. I whistle as I drive, realize I am doing exactly
what she has planned from the beginning. But feel no
bitterness, am content that she has won.

It is twilight when I reach the house in San Anselmo.
No answer to my knock, the bell sounds hollow, no car in
the garage. I peer through the windows, beat on the door.
At the back of the house I find an unlocked window, force

my way in. They are gone. I walk through every room looking for a note, though I know there will be none.

I drive then to Ariana's apartment on Telegraph Hill. My things are still there, her clothes are gone. No note. I feel a depression beginning, something being tied in a knot, pulled tight. I close the door of her apartment, close my heart, go back to my own place, turn the key.

XIV

Sometimes we suffer desperately, would do anything, try anything, but are lost, find no way. We cast about, distract ourselves, search, but find no connection between the misery we feel and the way we live. The pain comes from nowhere, gives no clue. We are bored, nothing has meaning; we become depressed. What to do? How to live? Something is wrong but we cannot imagine another way of living which would free us.

Yet there must be a way, for no sustained feeling can exist as a thing in itself, independent of what we do. If the suffering is serious and intractable it must be intimately and extensively connected, in ways we do not perceive, with the way we live. We have to look for such connections. Sometimes there is nothing to be done until they are found.

Therapy may help. One may discover, for example, a simmering hatred of one's wife, not consciously felt, not expressed, but turned against one's self, experienced as depression. Such a finding may still not indicate what one should do; for that will depend on yet other feelings, connections, implications. Should one begin to express the anger? Perhaps, if the grievance is reasonable and if there is also affinity and love. Should one get a divorce? Perhaps, if there is not even that minimum affection necessary for trying to work out differences. Sometimes there is no love, and good reason for hatred, and still one does not want a divorce: then one must be struck by this curious thing, that one clings to a source of frustration and torment, must ask why, and perhaps only then may begin to uncover a profound dependence which has been both well hidden by, and fully expressed in, the hostile tie. One hates her but can't leave her because one is afraid. Afraid of what? And why? What one should do may come to be known only after this dependence is examined in its relations with various other feelings and experiences. Sometimes there is no grievance and much love, and then, gradually, one may learn that he scapegoats his wife and may realize that he must, therefore, be needing to feel hatred, that he is using it for ulterior purposes—perhaps to cover up feelings of inadequacy, so avoiding the awareness of what he might want to do if he weren't afraid.

Much of our suffering is just so obscure as this. Frigidity, social anxiety, isolation, boredom, disaffection with life—in all such states we may see no correlation between the inner feeling and the way we live. Yet no such feeling can be independent of behavior; and if only we find the connections we may begin to see how a change in the way we live will make for a change in the way we feel.

Since freedom depends upon awareness, psychotherapy may, by extending awareness, create freedom. When in therapy a life story of drift and constraint is reworked to expose alternatives for crucial courses of action, asking always "Why did you do that?" attaching doubt to every explanation which is cast in the form of necessary reaction to antecedent cause, always reminding the patient that "Even so . . . it was possible to have acted otherwise"—in all this one is rewriting the past, is taking the story of a life which was experienced as shaped by circumstance and which was so recounted, and retelling it in terms of choice and responsibility. As a court may remind a defendant that ignorance of the law is no excuse, so a therapist may remind a patient that blindness to freedom does not justify constraint. And insofar as it may come to seem credible to rewrite one's life in terms of ignored choice, to assume responsibility retrospectively for what one has done and so has become, it will become possible likewise to see alternatives in the present, to become aware that one is free now in this moment to choose how to live, and that what one will become will follow upon what he now does.

When, however, in therapy a life story is reworked to expose the forces which "drove" one to do as he did, emphasizing traumas which twisted him and shaped defenses, hidden constraints situational and libidinal which required that he react in the way he did and in no other—in all this, too, one is rewriting the past, is taking a story which must have contained some elements of freedom and responsibility and retelling it in terms of causes lying outside one's control, so teaching the patient to see himself as the product of inner and outer forces. Where he feels himself to be the author of action, his analysis will show him as object being acted upon. He comes then to regard himself as being lived by unknown and largely unknowable forces. As consolation prize he may acquire the capacity to guess at the nature of those obscure forces that move him. But only guess. He must not attempt seriously to bear witness to that which, by definition, he cannot know. He must remain forever the dilettante, making modest conjecture at the gusts which blow him this way and that. He becomes not only an object but opaque, most necessarily to himself.

A "completely analyzed" person is one who has been treated for many years by an orthodox analyst. When such a one breaks down and is hospitalized we are surprised; if the patient is himself a psychoanalyst we are shocked. Our reaction bespeaks the assumption that thorough analysis resolves all serious inner conflict, that thereafter—though one may expect times of sadness, uncertainty, and unrest—these will derive from reality conflicts and so will not lead to breakdown. There is little to support such a view; indeed, the most cursory glance at three generations of analysts leaves it in tatters. The surprise we feel when a "well analyzed" person breaks down derives from our wish to view man as a machine. Very delicate and complicated, to be sure, like a fine watch, and liable therefore to subtle, tricky problems of adjustment which may require the lengthy services of an expert; but when finally we get rid of all the bugs we may expect smooth and reliable function. Such an image of man is at odds with what we know life to be. If we seriously regard our private thought and feeling, our visions at night when the wind blows, when rain falls on a deserted island, then—though fine adjustments have been made by a great watchmaker—we find so much conflict, misery, confusion, that we know we are never through and never safe. The suffering and the danger cannot be left behind. They are what we are. Psychoanalysis does not qualify anyone to live in the kingdom of heaven, only helps in the effort to change in such a way as to deal better with emerging conflicts which will never end so long as we live. Indeed, since we who undertake analysis are those who have more than average trouble with inner conflict, we may receive considerable help—quite enough to justify the undertaking—and still end up with more misery than those who have not been analyzed.

In reconstructing a life story truth is necessary but not sufficient. Truth does not demarcate, cannot determine whether we should dwell upon cause or choice. Two histories of the same life may be radically different, yet equally true. If we have failed an examination we may say, "I would not have failed if the teacher had not asked that question on Cromwell—which, after all, had not come up in class," or "I would not have failed if I had studied harder." Both statements are addressed to the same experience, in the same effort to understand; both claim to answer the question "Why did I fail?" and both may be true. Truth does not here provide the criterion for selection; the way we understand the past is determined, rather, by the future we desire. If we want to excuse ourselves we elect the former view; if we want to avoid such failures in the future we elect the latter. (If we believe our aim to be the passing of such exams in the future, and if we nevertheless elect the former view of the present failure, then we are confused.)

Likewise in addressing ourselves to the failure of a lifetime, and asking why, we may arrive at answers significantly different but equally true. In the life most free and most aware, so much defining action still occurs without choice that it is always feasible to compose an accurate and cogent account in terms of genes, drives, and circumstance. Conversely, in the life most crushed by outside force, there nevertheless exists the potentiality for actions other than those in fact taken. With the noose around our neck there still are options—to curse God or to pray, to weep or to slap the executioner in the face.

Of two equally true accounts of the same life the one we choose will depend upon the consequences we desire, the future we intend to create. If the life is our own or one of our patients, if it involves suffering and there is desire to change, we will elect a history written in terms of choice; for this is the view that insists upon the awareness of alternatives, the freedom to make one's self into something different. If the life in question is one we observe from a distance, without contact or influence, for example a life which has ended, we may elect a history written in terms of cause. In reconstructing a life that ended at Auschwitz we usually ignore options for other courses of individual behavior, locate cause and responsibility with the Nazis; for our intent is not to appraise the extent to which one person realized existing opportunity, but to examine and condemn the social evil which encompassed and doomed him. In considering the first eighteen years in the life of Malcolm X few of us would find much point in formulating his progress from delinquency to rackets to robbery to prison in terms of choice, holding him responsible for not having transcended circumstance; most of us would find the meaning of his story to lie in the manner in which racism may be seen as the cause of his downward course.

Conflict, suffering, psychotherapy—all these lead us to look again at ourselves, to look more carefully, in greater detail, to find what we have missed, to understand a mystery; and all this extends awareness. But whether this greater awareness will increase or diminish freedom will depend upon what it is that we become aware of. If the greater awareness is of the causes, traumas, psychodynamics that "made" us what we are, then we are understanding the past in such a way as to prove that we "had" to become what we are; and, since this view applies equally to the present which is the unbroken extension of that determined past, therapy becomes a way of establishing why we must continue to be what we have been, a way of disavowing choice with the apparent blessing of science, and the net effect will be a decrease in freedom. If, however, the greater awareness is of options unnoticed, of choices denied, of other ways to live, then freedom will be increased, and with it greater responsibility for what we have been, are, and will become.

XV

After a few days I call her friends; no one knows where they are. "That's the way they leave," Ellen says, "every two or three years they come back, are part of the scene, you begin to count on them; then they've gone, no one knows why or where, no announcement, no farewell parties. They'll be back. But in the meantime, darling . . . come see me."

I don't try to find her, I've had enough. All her life she will be responsible for Scott as for a defective child. Divorcing him, if she ever does, will make no difference. Better it end now. Maybe I'm lucky. If I had actually moved in, tried to treat Scott . . . what a mess. Sheer good fortune it was too late. I nurture a sense of scorn.

If there were anything special, any magic to exempt our love from the attrition of living, I would go after her. It seems there is but I can't believe it. It had a magical phase, was interrupted before the magic ran out. That's all. A little more time and it would fall into the rancor and resignation of all old loves.

I think of following her, of telephoning, devise ways to find her. I have the name of a friend in New York, of her aunt in Switzerland, the post office or her bank may know. Sometimes I pick up the phone to find out, but put it back. Sometimes in the evening I catch myself in reveries of search, pursuing her through mazes, over obstacles.

No search is necessary. After two weeks comes a letter from Zürich. "Dearest, don't be angry, I had to go. Don't be jealous; I love no one but you, am your wife in every way but name. Don't be sad, I'll come back. Don't forget me."

A week later a letter from Mürren. Scott is photographing the mountains. "This is the first time," she writes, "I have a minute alone. Usually he stays at my side like a child, moving with me from one part of the room to another." So of course, I think bitterly, he has to be with her at night, that's when fears are worst, cuddled up close to ward off night terrors, and she must comfort him . . . any way she can. "It's marvelous to have these few hours alone. I walk in the mountains with such longing for you. It's so beautiful and I so much want to be here with you. Will we? one day? Please believe in us. Look over this bad time, promise me something. I promise you everything. Scott will get over this dependence, will find someone else. I can hardly wait. Then there's nothing I won't do for you . . . go anywhere, do anything. Don't forget me. Help me hold on to our chance.

"We are going on to Zermatt tomorrow. Scott is terribly restless. We stay nowhere more than a few days. He has bought a powerful sports car, likes to drive, needs to be doing something, have something in his hands. We roar from town to town, demons are chasing him. Don't know how long in Zermatt. Write to me darling."

I write letters but don't send them. Anything casual seems insulting, and I can't bring myself to say flat out, "It's over, forget it."

A letter from Zermatt: "Darling. You must be so angry with me. Can't you forgive me? I'm desolate you may not love me, may not want me any more. Write me. Tell me I can come back."

Her last letter is from Paris: "We're still rushing about, place to place, here to there. Scott is not working, is always with me, clinging. I don't know how long I can go on. I'm very sad . . . in this gay city."

So—how to get over being in love? Everyone recovers, you shouldn't have to work at it. Like losing a religion, it's something that overtakes you sooner or later, but I'm not willing to wait, want it over now. I'm hurting and in a hurry.

Every hour there comes to my office someone who has enveloped me in an aura of goodness, charm, insight; compounded of memory and need but perceived as my real quality, my very self. They are spellbound but not by me, flounder and gasp in nets of their own weaving. I too. Have put myself in thrall to her. Of what is it made? An invisible garment of longing, fitting like skin, but I know it's raiment. If I could somehow catch hold of it, twist it over my head and off, I would be free. But when I try I seize my flesh, it's my very self I tear.

I transport myself five years hence: am taking my ease on a terrace overlooking a tropical beach, sipping dark rum, becoming interested in the pretty woman half hidden in the huge raffia chair, reading *Réalités,* swinging a bare leg. I think of the effortless detachment, even amusement, with which I will then look back on this madness. How hasten that state? What will I know then I don't know now? Over and over I strain at the invisible garment, but can't slip out.

I study past loves for instruction. They fitted as tightly. My wife . . . but we were so young, unknowing, so much more driven by insecurities than pulled by love. There was a girl once, I never touched her but felt this torment. Driving by her house at night, looking up at the lighted window, seeing her come and go, waiting at one in the morning for her to return from a date, sweater over her shoulders, the burst of jealousy—would he go in?—driving around the block to see. I knew it was crazy—she was nineteen, I could have been her father—but could not dispel it, could but hold it at bay. She moved away. Don't know how or when it faded, feel nothing now, can look back and see her as she was—a shy college girl, serious, a slow smile, majoring in political science. And how will I one day see Ariana? I begin to paint the diminished image: a pretty woman, a good heart, loyal, leave out all the magic . . . but then am struck down by longing, the brush clatters to the floor.

I see her distortion better than my own. How little do I esteem my colleagues, how frequently find them petty, selfish, dull. Yet with what keen appreciation have I often viewed myself. Now I think how much I'm like them: and finding so little to admire in them I find equally for myself. I feel a sinister restlessness, smell my death on the wind, need a task.

Sometimes I fall under a spell, think we have a unique affinity, she and I, something different in kind, and that nothing out of the past can tell me anything about it. But this is a siren song, this way lies shipwreck. The whole endeavor of my life is the study of emotion, of love and hate, of the needs, drives, and dependencies that bind people together and drive them apart; and every transcendent relationship—my own, my friends', my patients'—has shown itself in time to transcend nothing, to be reducible to the everyday, generally dirty elements of which we are so fallibly made; and the greater the transcendent frenzy the greater the fall. Indeed sanity means primarily just this capacity to deny transcendence, to accept that we are compounded of sex and aggression and self-love—with just enough caring left over to get our children through childhood and so to continue the species. Ecstasy is narcissism, deathless love is delusion, worship of God is fear of death.

I force myself to go out socially. Women become available but in bed I can't make it or, when I can, am prey to dragons of guilt, of loathing for myself—as if I owe fidelity to a mistress who cavorts about the world with her libertine husband. Two people mention having heard from Ariana, say she asked about me.

Sometime in these three months—I don't know when, didn't notice—I must have given up, become unable or unwilling to fight the obsession. It begins to make me sick. My life changes. I stop going out, see no one but patients. When my work day is over I sit and drink and watch the sun go down, fall in a trance. Stories occur effortlessly. Ariana and I have children, walk on beaches, in streets of foreign cities, lie locked together in strange hotel rooms, create a past together, live out a future. At times I lose her, search over the world, struggle and die. Reveries pass into dreams, dreams into nightmares from which I wake in terror and sweat. I lose weight; from the mirror my face looks back gray; from the couch I hear that my colleagues say I'm sick. Friends intervene, press invitations. I have no heart for anything. One day I hear myself saying, "No, I can't," to a woman who wants only a consultation. I return no calls, tell my answering service to accept no messages, terminate several patients.

One afternoon I go to the waiting room for my next patient, find her gone. Her handbag is on the chair, she must have stepped out for something. A few minutes later she still has not returned. I see a note on the floor, pick it up: "Dear Dr. Archer, I may be too sleepy to finish this. I forgot . . ." This is Mrs. Laine: she has probably gone home to get something; meanwhile has forgotten her purse. I take it in my office. Ten minutes pass. I pick up her note again, the writing is firm. She was going to write something she meant to tell me, I surmise, but was reminded of something else; picked up her car keys, which probably lay beside her purse, forgot the purse, drove home. I look at my watch. Thirty minutes past her time. I telephone her home; she's not there, the maid thinks she's gone to her doctor. I look through her purse: money, lipstick, letters, tickets, combs, compact. No bottles, nothing suspicious. I telephone her husband at his office on Montgomery Street; he has no idea where she is, implies I should not be troubling him. I think of Ariana. Where is she? What is she doing? Images flutter up. I stifle them, don't want to care.

Mrs. Laine's hour is over. I call her house again; she has not returned. It's unimportant. She's not so depressed, wouldn't kill herself. Anyway, I don't care. . . . This startles me, I feel ashamed. I go to the waiting room for my next patient, change my mind, cancel the hour.

Now I start to work on the whereabouts of Mrs. Laine. If she took barbiturates where, if not home, might she go? What might she have remembered? . . . Maybe something in connection with her daughter. I telephone the daughter, no answer. If she were driving from my office to her daughter's home, how would she go? Through the Presidio. In my car I follow her presumptive route. A bus swings wide around a corner, picks up speed, hurtles toward me on the wrong side of the street, swerves away with but inches to spare. I see a look of implacable hatred on the pale taut face of the driver, think of him piloting that huge missile through these crowded streets, hating all he meets.

I go on, wanting very much to find the sad forgetful woman.

Her black station wagon is parked neatly at the side of the road near the Twenty-fifth Street exit. She is lying on the front seat, head rolled oddly to one side, mouth open. I call her name, no answer; put my hand on her shoulder, she doesn't move; shake her slightly. Her lips are cracked, filmed with dry mucus. I lift an eyelid, the eye rolls up, the skin is beaded with sweat. There is a note on the floor: "Dear Dr. Archer. I don't know whether I can stay awake. I forgot . . ." The words disappear in illegible scrawls. I drive her to the hospital, stay while her stomach is emptied.

At Clive's request the research group listens to the last analytic hour. It is tedium: the tape is faulty, Mrs. Laine had been mumbling, there were many silences. I describe the attempted suicide, her present condition.

It is a still gray day. Fog hangs motionless over the rooftops outside the psychoanalytic institute. Large drops of water form on eaves, fall in slow irregular drip. I look at my colleagues and wait. Lars is hunched over the table, head sunk between massive shoulders, scowling inwardly, eyebrows drawn together, forehead wrinkled vertically. Clive leans back in his chair, detached, preoccupied. Julian glances about, makes contact, analyzes the suicide attempt in terms of oral dependence and regression. Clive becomes impatient, interrupts. His face looks thinner these days, grayer, glasses flash blindly as he lifts his head in autocratic scorn, has become the pedant, does not converse but indoctrinates, has the final word, casts it down from superior height. "A first-year resident could have seen this coming."

"A first-year resident," I say, "would have available a set

of certainties I don't have."

Nothing can touch him. "I submit," he says, "that this attempt would not have occurred had the confrontation with the irrationality of her anger been combined with an interpretation of its origin in childhood."

"That's meaningless," Lars says. "There's no way to test it."

Clive turns slowly on Lars. "It rests," he says "on proven clinical principles."

"Such as what?"

"That one must not force a patient to internalize more anger than he can handle."

"What's 'more than he can handle'? for Christ's sake!" Lars says. "How do you measure it? How can you tell what quantity of anger is going to be released by any one intervention? And how can you ever know, until it's too late, whether that amount, itself immeasurable, is going to be more than a patient can handle?"

Lars looks down at the white knuckles of clenched hands, beats ponderously against the table top. Clive glances about as if asking the rest of us to agree that the refutation of such nonsense is unnecessary, beneath his dignity; but can't contain himself, sits forward, gesticulates, shakes his head. "I don't agree, I don't agree. . . ."

And on and on until our time is up. Clive looks at his watch, moves irritably. For several moments there is no sound but the irregular drip of water. I say nothing, the conference ends like a stream in the desert.

In my office, nighttime, I find myself waiting, for whom I don't know. I read magazines, write letters to almost forgotten friends. At ten I begin listening to the tape of the conference, take notes, prepare to dictate a summary; wander through scraps of memory and music, people, happenings; circling, coming back always to Ariana—what is she doing? where are they? I turn off the light, lie on my analytic couch in darkness. A dull light appears gradually at the window; the sky is covered with a motionless film of cloud, behind it somewhere a moon. There is no wind, but a leaden stillness and the slow drip of water.

I don't need to listen to that tape: I know what they said, have heard it all before, many times, can say it for them; feel nausea for the analysis, the whole project, for all our endless talk, the straining at science with precise formulations applied to the uncontrolled and uncontrollable variables of a human life.

I think of Lars, at home probably, pacing about his house in that ponderous way, bloodshot little eyes, anguished, watery, the broad face; the slow swinging of heavy arms, the beating together of hands, turning, house shaking to his tread, on and on, like a tiger in a cage. And Julian? What is he doing? Something for himself, something for pleasure . . . scheming for more money. And Clive? . . . in his study sitting at a Spanish table, wearing a green corduroy jacket, bending over his papers; his wife comes in wearing a housecoat, brings a thermos of tea, retires; and there he will sit till one o'clock, contriving traps to snare some final truth about the soul, of which nothing is final.

I see Ariana's face on the gray screen of the window, hear her voice against the drip of water, watch her following after Scott, around and around some unknown room in an unknown country, black hair getting loose on the white neck, hairpins dropping, wringing her hands, suffering his gibes.

And I? . . . Lying on an analytic couch—my own, no

one behind me, no analyst, no God—analyzing myself in a
dark and empty room, ideas chasing around the blind
labyrinth, running into the same dead ends, while I look
out on the still, dripping night, heart beating every second
for—how much longer? ten minutes? years?—and how will I
spend it? Like this probably, in impulse and bafflement,
some rare escapes. Always something left over. Define it, it
flees the definition before the ink is dry.

Mrs. Laine survives. I spend much time with her at the
hospital. "The worst that can happen if you try," I tell
her, "is to fail. And the most final failure is to die. So if
you try—take all the risks—the worst that can happen is
what you were bringing on yourself. How much better to
let death happen if it will while your hand is raised to
something else."

Treating her effort at suicide, I treat my own, find I'm as
forgetful as she, am forgetting to live. If I bury my feeling
for Ariana, I bury myself; if I insist on living only by what
I know, I insist on dying. I feel a veering. The captain of
the ship—with clear eye and long experience, knowing of
rocks and shoals—takes his hands off the wheel. Deep
currents fix the course.

XVI

I cable her in Paris, no reply. I telephone the Hotel
Normandie, speak to the concierge. They left a month ago;
she has written three times for mail—from Nice, Geneva,
Vienna. He's pulling her around like a madman. I
telephone the Hotel Sacher in Vienna: they left a week
ago, no forwarding address. I telephone Ariana's friend in
New York, who doesn't know, then her aunt in Bern, who
is away. Her bank is no help, nor the post office. Scott's
lawyer doesn't know, nor his family in Detroit. I begin to
feel baffled, cable her at American Express in a number of
cities at random, make flight reservations to Vienna, then
cancel. What would I do there? Where would a detective
begin? Perhaps here. I call every person I know to be
acquainted with her, send cables to every past address.
Several people are helping me. Two weeks pass and I have
no lead, spend most of my time on the phone. Suddenly I
think to try Eastman Kodak, Scott uses an ultrafine-grain
film. I telephone the special services department and
within minutes learn that a packet of film from him has
just come in—from the Hotel Baur au Lac in Zürich.

I telephone at ten in the morning. The circuits are busy,
it's three hours before I get through, then no one answers
in their room. I keep trying, eventually at one in the
morning, Zürich time, Scott is on the phone. "Oh, hello
Max." He sounds weak, far away.

"Let me speak to Ariana."

"She's not here."

"Where is she?"

There is a pause. "In the hospital."

"What's the matter?"

"I . . . d-d-don't know," he says vaguely.

"Well, tell me what happened."

"She had some fever. Not much."

"Don't hold out on me, Scott. Tell me something. What does the doctor say?"

"He doesn't know either. Says she's toxic. Is going to make some tests. L-l-look . . . it's not serious, Max. She'll be out in a day or two."

"What hospital is it?"

A pause. "I don't know."

"What do you mean you don't know?"

"The name. I called the American consul, he suggested this hospital. But I don't know the name. I can give you the address."

"God damn it, Scott, give me the name. There's a phone book right beside you. Look it up!"

"What do you need it for?"

"I want to call her."

"Oh, you couldn't do that anyway," he says with relief. "There's no phone in her room."

"What's the name of her doctor?"

"I don't know."

I start to threaten, catch myself. Connection is not yet made. "How come you don't know his name?" I say easily.

"I've just talked to him once. She went in today. I've got his name written somewhere."

Again a pause. I decide to push no further. "And how are you, Scott?"

"Oh, fine . . . fine." He sounds scared, the same voice I heard at the tea table with the yellow brocade cloth, hysteria that may rise any moment, boil over into panic.

"Scott, will you give her a message?"

"What? Oh yes . . . sure."

"Tell her I called, I hope she'll be well soon."

"Sure, sure . . . I'll tell her."

In two hours I am on a plane to New York, six hours later am leaving Kennedy Airport on Swissair for Zürich; at three in the afternoon I walk up to the desk of the Baur au Lac and learn that Mr. Craig checked out that morning. No forwarding address. I talk to the concierge, mail clerk, doorman, porter, chambermaid; learn nothing except, from the doorman, that Mr. Craig left alone in a dark blue Facel Vega, asked no directions. I go to the American consul, who remembers the call, tells me he gave Scott the name of a Dr. Weber at the University Hospital. At the hospital I'm told Mrs. Craig was discharged that morning. Dr. Weber is in; after waiting an hour I am able to see him—a tall man, narrow face with dark skin, hooked nose, gray hair, slender except for a round belly covered by a double-breasted waistcoat. He speaks English with slight accent, accepts me as colleague and friend of the family. He doesn't know where they have gone. She was released against his advice, on her husband's insistence. She didn't seem to care, but her husband was anxious. She was not so sick, he says, that he felt it necessary to insist. A little fever, had lost weight, some weakness, more depressed than ill. No interest, nothing to say, no complaints. "Too bad you didn't come sooner," Dr. Weber says. "Maybe you could have helped. I had in mind a psychiatric consultation if the tests came back negative." I ask if there was any talk of where to go, he said none. Any mention of places or names? None. Where to send the bill? Scott paid in cash. A home address for the record? Baur au Lac.

I telephone the principal hotels, inquire at the tourist

bureau, check again with the American consulate. Nothing. I decide to stay the night while considering how to proceed, take a room at the Baur au Lac. In the evening I walk through the Arboretum along the Zürich-See—a clear, balmy night, stars and mountains reflected in black water, excursion boats moving back and forth, music, people promenading, can hardly bear she's so near and sick but unreachable. At ten o'clock I return to the hotel, ask for messages. None. I am the only passenger in the elevator, the operator is a man I had not seen that afternoon. "Do you remember," I ask, "an American couple who stayed here? Dark-haired woman, slight gray-haired man? The woman went to the hospital a couple of days ago, the man checked out today."

"Oh yes . . . I heard someone was asking."

"Do you know where they went?"

"No. . . ."

"Anything?"

" . . . Only he asked me this morning how far to Interlaken." We arrive at my floor.

"Take me down again," I say.

At the desk I ask about hotels in Interlaken, go back to my room with a list, find them on the third call—the Beau Rivage. "No, no," I say to the operator at the Beau Rivage, "don't ring—don't mention this call. I want to surprise them."

I can find no car to rent at this hour, call here and there, finally locate a cab driver who will take me. At two in the morning we set forth. The driver says we'll be there by seven. At five o'clock, a few kilometers past Sachseln, we hit an oil-slick and go in a drainage ditch knee-deep in water. The trunk of the cab contains no tool for digging. We gather sticks and stones, force them under the wheels.

As the driver attempts to pull out, the car tilts, appears about to fall on its side. He is unwilling to try further, says we have to wait. I protest but he ignores me, sits on a rock, lights his pipe. The first car to approach slows as I wave a handkerchief, then apparently is frightened of two men, speeds on. The second car, bearing a German license, does not even hesitate. After a half hour an ancient wheezing truck with a load of unbaled hay stops. The cab driver arranges for the farmer to send back a wrecker from Brienz. I pay the cab driver, ride with the farmer to Brunig, where he is to stop for a while before going on to Brienz. In Brunig I can find no taxi. It's now eight o'clock, I'm afraid I'll lose them. I telephone the hotel, ask for Mrs. Craig. There is some delay, then the phone is ringing in their room. "Hello."

"Hello, Scott. Let me speak to Ariana, please."

"Yes . . . what is it?" He sounds breathless.

"Scott! Let me speak to Ariana."

"No, no thank you."

"Scott! Put her on! Ariana!" I am shouting, hoping she is near the phone, will hear me through his stalling.

"No . . . no, thank you," he says. "We'll come down to breakfast."

"God damn you!" I yell in the now-dead phone.

I try again, the hotel line is busy. I get through five minutes later, am told by the hotel operator that Mr. and Mrs. Craig are accepting no calls. I catch a ride finally on a dairy truck. It's a quarter of ten when I reach the Beau Rivage. They have checked out.

Again I inquire of desk, doorman, concierge, again no word of where they have gone, or which direction. The switchboard operator looks at me curiously. I go out in the town, rent a car, get maps, come back, sit in the dining room, order coffee. "Did you," I ask the waiter, "see the American couple who left this morning?"

"In the Facel Vega?"

"Yes."

"I waited on them. They sat here, where you sit."

"Did they say where they were going."

"No. The man was in a hurry, would not eat, just coffee. Spoke of leaving. The woman said nothing."

"Did you hear any place . . . any town?"

"No. Nothing."

They were here, I think, when my second call got through. I see the switchboard from where I sit. It would have been so easy for Ariana to be called. Scott, I imagine, came into the dining room with her, excused himself, gave the operator some money along with the instruction that they were "accepting no calls."

Beside me is a mirror. I am forty-eight hours without sleep, see a stubble of beard, red eyes, gray face, suddenly am sick with fatigue; think of taking a room, sleeping, but am pushed on by her presence just two hours ago in this chair, in some anguish of longing perhaps, wondering will we ever meet again—while across the lobby, at the end of a wire blocked by a ten-franc note, I was straining to reach her.

I open the map. Four ways to leave Interlaken. He would not go back toward Brienz and Zürich. Lauterbrunnen is a dead end. So—one of the two roads west around the Thuner-See. I guess the south shore, finish my coffee, prepare to go. The waiter is standing at the desk talking to the clerk. He turns, points at me. I motion to him. "Check, please," I say when he comes to the table.

"Sir . . . was it . . . Craig?"

"Yes. . . ."

"Your friends . . . Mr. and Mrs. Craig?"

"Yes. Why?"

"There's been an accident . . ." Pity appears on his face. ". . . the lady is dead."

The doorman gives me directions. A wrecker passes towing the Facel Vega, the front end smashed back, windshield gone. "It will take hours to move the bus," the doorman says. "The road is blocked."

At the hospital I am shown into a white examining room; the body, covered, lies on a stretcher. I pull down the sheet—start back with a cry. A sword blade of glass has been driven through her head. The left side of her face is lacerated, legs broken. The blue eyes are open, dry, a film of dust from the road. She wears a straw-colored suit of knitted silk. I know it well, have seen it cling to her form, move with her motion, rise with her breathing—now black with oil and blood. I put my hands on her, she is not yet cold, throw myself upon her, lift her head, sob, cut my forehead on the glass that pierces hers, kiss her cheek, eyes. . . . There is a rumble, a gurgling, then a smell: her bowels have moved. Her hands are untouched—brown, delicate. The fingers are getting stiff. I fold them on her breast, close the lids on the dusty eyes, lift the sheet over the impaled head.

Scott has a concussion, broken ribs and arm, is in shock. I call Ariana's aunt, Mrs. Lamanet, in Bern; she comes that night. The next day Scott's father arrives from Detroit. He is allowed to see his son, on returning says to me, "I think he is out of his mind. He was hiding under the bed. Didn't seem to know Ariana was dead."

"He knows," I say.

Scott refuses to see me, is put under heavy narcosis. The doctors say he is in "traumatic delirium."

The next day Mr. Craig, Mrs. Lamanet, and I attend the burial. The coffin is borne by a horse-drawn wagon. We follow on foot up a narrow winding road to a small cemetery in a clearing. On one side is a sheer cliff, a rushing river below. A Lutheran minister in black with broad-brimmed hat reads the service; the coffin is lowered; each of us drops a bit of soil in the grave. The minister leaves, followed by Mr. Craig and Mrs. Lamanet. I stay. After a while there appears, as if from nowhere, a wizened old man with one eye, one tooth, and a wispy gray beard. He pays no attention to me, shovels dirt on the coffin with palsied hands, methodically fills the grave, stamps the mound, shuffles away.

The next day Mrs. Lamanet leaves. I drive nine kilometers to the site of the accident near Leissigen, see each turn of the road as she last saw it—though she may have looked down or inward, have seen nothing. Scott had swung wide on an inside curve, hit the right front end of an oncoming bus, the car had overturned and come to rest under a locust tree near the edge of the lake. There, in a patch of grass among the rocks, I find her blood. I go back every morning, sit there with my hand in the dark stain, while tourists pass on their way to Bern and Geneva. The afternoons I spend at her grave. The torrent speaks to me, I feel a surge of madness, want to tear away the earth.

On the fourth day Scott, still hallucinating, is taken by car with his father and two attendants to a hospital in Zürich. That night there is a storm. Lightning cracks around my turret room, thunder explodes across the valley, rain falls in livid sheets. I stand at the open window, the lead gutter overflows. In the intervals between thunder I hear the crash of water on rocks in the river. I lean out, strain toward that ledge where she lies, water streaming

162

down in black dirt, wanting to be chilled as she is, tears and rain on my face, thinking now . . . now it really is too late.

The next morning there is a bright sunshine. Under the locust tree there is no trace of her blood. Even the place is different, covered with a wash of gravel. At the cemetery I find the grave sunk three inches. A green and black snake slithers toward me, raises its head, red forked tongue darting in and out. I pick up a stone. There is a high wind, the trees spill flashing rainbows. From the cliff comes the roar of a cataract. I drop the stone, push back the pull of madness. The grave digger with one eye and one tooth is smoking a bamboo pipe. I drive to Zürich, catch a plane for home.